S[illegible]com

Toad

Charles Moberly

Tancava
PRESS

The Scrotum Toad

by Charles Moberly

All characters are purely fictional and exist only within the author's imagination and the chapters of this work.

ISBN

978-1-7398800-0-2 Paperback

978-1-7398800-1-9 e-book

Published by Tancava Press

https://charlesmoberlyauthor.blogspot.com/

CHAPTER ONE

Jake leant back in his chair and closed his eyes. He'd made his choice: *Waters of Eostre* in the African Republic of Zuzubia. Sitting at his computer, still smarting from his enforced resignation, he'd decided he wanted to go abroad, to cultivate the land, to feel the soil through his fingers and watch things - make things - grow. A concept of sustainable horticulture called permaculture seemed to be just what he was looking for.

The moment *Waters of Eostre* had come up on his laptop, Jake knew he'd found the right place. The picture on the home page taken from the air was stunning. Below the settlement, cultivated terraces slalomed down the hillside to a large river. To the left as one looked at the photo, an immense rock several hundred feet high acted as a buttress to the terraces and a turning point for the river, slinging it three quarters of the way round its flank so that it disappeared, gaining momentum as it went, its sluggish brown surface churning white. Other photos were equally enticing: of ponds, sculptures, thatched *rondavels* and groves of exotic fruit. Even better, *Waters of Eostre* was on the edge of a game park, just outside it technically, but the view from that rock included herds of grazing zebras and wildebeests.

But what had appealed to Jake most was the name of the owner, Tangwystl Breeze. There was a photo of her, handsome in a New Age way, with a defiantly straight nose and black witchy hair twining about her shoulders. Forty, perhaps a little older, too old for Jake, yet there was something about her which stirred him. It was certainly her name, because Jake had a thing about Welsh women ever since he'd had an ardent fling with a single mother. She'd driven him wild by being constantly unattainable while she juggled job, child and household; no time, no time, no stop it, not now, then suddenly and unpredictably turning to him with melting arms and performing wherever they happened to be. Stop the car, stop the car, here, now, or across the kitchen table. The affair hadn't lasted, but it had left Jake with a certainty that Welsh women were the most desirable and satisfying in the world. Names like Myfanwy, Bronwyn and Glenys would make his breath do funny things, and once he'd spluttered a mixture of red wine and cocktail sausage over a girl who'd introduced herself as Angharad.

Finding out that *Eostre* was the name of an obscure pagan goddess - pagan, druid, Celtic, Welsh - fuelled Jake's anticipation. He couldn't get out of his head the similarity to the word 'oestrogen' and therefore female sexuality, even though the spelling alone made the connection absurd.

That was how Jake became a woofer, a worker-volunteer on an organic farm, in the heart of Africa. How, but not completely why. Jake had been, and technically still was, a teacher. As a free thinker, and unfortunately for him a free speaker and doer, it had been inevitable that sooner or later he would collide with School Tradition. And what is more traditional than Christmas?

Putting Jake in charge of the school nativity play had been a mistake he'd been keen to exploit.

'Try and make it a bit different this year.' The Head had drawn together her brows and sphinctered her lips. It always seemed to Jake that she was whistling a silent 'No-o' of disapproval just after she'd spoken to him. He wondered which of them loathed the other the most. 'You know, expand the range of biblical characters.'

It hadn't taken Jake long to think of an additional part. Herod played an important role in the Christmas story and would make an excellent hissable villain. He's behind you. Oh no he isn't. Oh yes he is. To the Wise Men, when you have seen the Child, bring me word of where He is so that I may...woo-hoo, wer-her. The kids'll love that. They'll scream their heads off.

It was disgust at the tackiness and materialism of Christmas following a visit to his local shopping centre in October that had made Jake abandon the idea of Herod in favour of a much more subversive character, Santa Claus.

A year earlier, before Jake had arrived, the Head had been appalled when the Chairman of the all-male Board of Governors had pointed out that every single teacher in Junior School was female. She bit her tongue when he added that, with over a fifth of the parents being single mothers, some of the children had no contact with male role models in the flesh. Jake could imagine the Head cringing at the words 'contact', 'male' and 'flesh'. So when a vacancy had arisen for a history and geography teacher for Years 1 and 2, Jake knew that the seething Head had been forced to interview male-only candidates.

Right from the start of Jake's interview, the Head had signalled that she was an off-the-scale feminist and religious bigot. Jake was bright and mentally agile.

'Who is your greatest hero?'

'Joan of Arc.'

'What do you draw on when you're under pressure?'

'My feminine side.'

Being a single denomination establishment, the school was pushed and driven to a state of fundamental sectarianism by the divinely active, funded by the helpless taxpayer, whether he or she was Christian, Muslim, Hindu, Atheist, Agnostic or whatever. The casualties were tolerance, creative thinking and educational enlightenment. It was a requirement that all teachers should not merely genuflect in the direction of the school's brand of Christianity, but should show an enthusiasm verging on the rabid. At his interview Jake had not only genuflected for all he was worth, he'd thumped the devotional drum. He'd laid into the growth of secularism and the decline of morality, even though he knew perfectly well, and would soon be observing daily, that professing believers were no more moral than the rest of society. The growth of secularism was serious, he'd piously intoned, *serious*, but could be overcome by the power of prayer. Fortunately for Jake, he'd been able to lace these views with quotations from the Bible. Less than a year before, he'd had a relationship with one of the parents, a single mother, the one whose Welshness had made such an impression. In order to get her son into the school, she and the boy had been forced to attend weekly church services, a charade she'd submitted to for the sake of the boy's education. Jake, thrilling at their shoulders touching while he breathed in her pheromones, was more than happy to accompany them. Although concentration on anything other than the object of his desire had been hard, these Sundays had enabled Jake to pick up sufficiently resonant quotations from the New Testament to impress the Head at his interview. Clearly this young man was a believer, or else as good a bullshitter as she was. Either way, he got the job.

Rehearsals for the nativity play had been going to

plan. When the Wise Men peered into the crib, Jake had instructed them to leap back, so that Baby Jesus could sit up and squeak, 'Have a nice day', an opportunity for the chorus to sing, 'Sincerely, 'cerely, we don't think so, we don't care'. When the audience had recovered from that and had been lulled into thinking that this might after all be a conventional performance, Santa would burst into the room booming, 'Sweets for everyone, sweets and toys, expensive ones.'

Even Jake hadn't predicted the effect this would have on young siblings in the audience. As sweets cascaded across the floor, a fearsome pack of three- and four-year-olds, followed by their anxious mothers, charged the stage, leaving a few bewildered grandparents in their seats. Jake then had one of the shepherds ask innocently, 'What have we done to deserve this?' Jake had wanted Josh, who was playing Santa, to pause at this point so that the audience would be expecting him to reply something like, 'Because you've been good little children.' But he'd known that Josh would be far too excited on the night and would rush his lines. He did so, roaring back, 'Because you're worth it, ho-ho-ho.'

Children of course are unpredictable. As Jake was to relate to Kirsten at *Waters of Eostre* six months later, the shepherds turned to gaze in wonder as little Tamara, dressed as a star, scurried far too fast across the stage to hover over the crib. She stared at the audience. 'I want a wee-wee.'

'Don't tell me you stopped her going and she...'

'Not at all. I halted the play immediately so she could leave the room.'

'So what was the problem?'

'It was what I shouted out.'

'Which was?'

'Tinkle, tinkle, little star.'

Jake sat in the Head's office the next morning trying to look contrite.

'Why were all three kings boys?'

'For the same reason as Joseph was.'

'Don't you know we have a gender-neutral policy here?'

Jake made no comment.

'And Abdul was given the part of a camel?'

'His parents...'

'The rear end?'

'His parents didn't want Abdul to be directly part of the Christian story, but the boy himself didn't want to be left out.'

'Couldn't you find a Muslim part and build it in? They're both Abrahamic religions, you know,' she sniffed, as though Jake didn't.

It was then that he lost his temper, fatally. 'Next time I'll make sure he's in a Mohammed mask and then we can have a fatwa and a jihad followed by a stoning'.

Four months later, Jake was a woofer at *Waters of Eostre.* The place was everything he'd hoped it would be.

'Hi, I'm Tangle.'

Tangle? She's meant to be Tangwystl. But it didn't matter what had happened to Tangwystl, because the way she sang her name was as Welsh as sunlight on anthracite or a lamb in a valley with daffodils and leeks in the background. Tangle, with all the emphasis on the 'g'. Tangle, a Welsh harp tintinnabulating in the heart of Africa.

CHAPTER TWO

Kirsten sat at her computer, exhausted but triumphant. She'd just got the results of her degree in zoology and had been awarded First Class Honours. Now all she wanted was to get back to her native Denmark, spend a few weeks with her parents and fly to the small African Republic of Zuzubia, where she would start her research project on reptiles and amphibians. She couldn't wait to get there. She was looking forward to it excitedly, desperately, but now she was so tired. All she wanted was a quick and easy flight from London to Copenhagen.

It seemed so simple. A flight leaving Luton at 11.35 the next day: cost £2.99. She wouldn't have to get up ridiculously early and she'd be at her parents' house by the time it got dark. One adult single, £2.99: that's cheap. Seat allocation? Don't mind. Short flight, let them choose the seat, then I won't have to pay any extra. No, it won't let me do that, I have to choose a seat. All right, 9A, window. No, that's reserved for Loyal Super Bonus Customers only. Try another, 16A. £10. What? That's a rip off. I'll take it as a little reward for my qualification. Hold baggage? Unfortunately, yes. Accumulated baggage, very apt after four years in England. One large suitcase. Allowance 14kg. That's a bit mean, I'll be way over.

Kirsten left her screen and stood gazing at her half-packed suitcase with a mixture of nostalgia and apprehension. She'd already bought presents for her parents: some Portmeirion pottery and an antique vase. Silly really; they were far too heavy and she would have to cocoon them in clothes. She closed the case and carried it carefully to the bathroom, lowering it onto the scales. 12.2 kg. That's under the allowance but it's only half full. It's going to be more like 20. Too bad. How much do they charge for being overweight? £50, that's reasonable. No it's... what? They must be joking. £50 is the charge for each bag regardless of weight. How much if it's over? Another £50; hm, not so bad. No, wait a minute, it's £50 for every kilo over 14. For 20kg, that's 6 overweight. 6 £50s are, *lort*, £300. I'll have to throw some things out, that means give them away to that Uzbek or whatever he is who begs on the corner outside. I'd better aim for 18kg. That's 4 over, 4 £50s, that's £200 plus the £50 for having the hold luggage in the first place. What am I up to? £2.99 plus £10 plus £50 plus £200, total £262.99. Not bad for a £2.99 flight.

Would I like priority boarding for another £10? *For helvede!* No I fucking would not. Oh shit, I've pressed accept by accident. What's this? Would I like a badge to boast that I'm a priority boarder? Oh yes, and can it please say I'm a rich bitch and can afford it? Well I'm not, I'm a poor Danish student - no, graduate now - so cancel that. Just let me complete the booking.

Kirsten stared dreamily into space. Would I like to pay £5 for the stewardess to smile at me? Would I fuck. And pay another £5 for her to say, 'Have a Great Flight.' What would happen if I asked for 'Have a Great Flight' without the smile? That would be interesting. Would it be hissed through gritted teeth? I could stand there blocking the entrance, refusing to move into the aircraft, charming her with my own smile until she cracked. It would be rather fun. Reluctantly she returned to reality. Complete the booking, get it over with if I can without a supplement for saying no thank you to the duty-free goods and another no thank you to the donation to the charity of the airline's choosing, because they are so-o generous with other people's money. And £100 for going to the loo.

No, none of those. Travel insurance? £40? Ignore. It won't let me ignore. You moronic Danish graduate with your first class degree, how can you be so stupid? You have to say yes or no. Do I need it? Perhaps it's best now that I'm a top academic. Yes. £40. Thank you very much. New total £302.99.

A new message, 'Congratulations! You've just saved £138.00 on this booking!' How do they get that? *Rend mig!* Do they charge for logging off?

'Congratulations!' They're free with those, they're the only things that are free. 'You have just become eligible to join our elite club of Loyal Super

Bonus Customers. For a once-only joining fee of just £150, you can collect 1 point for every £5 you spend with us. Just look at our superlative offers.' Oo, do let's. 'Collect 1,000 points and you can purchase a unique Pucci watch for only £99.99 or a fabulous Chemise bag for £149.99.' So that you can pay £50 to take it on the plane and £50 a kilo to stuff it. *Dit rovhul!*

Kirsten had never hit a computer before and she would never do so again. *Kneppe!* Her laptop went dead.

A month later she stood halfway along the track which meandered gently downwards from her new home to the main cluster of buildings at *Waters of Eostre*. It was late afternoon, still hot but with a balmy softness which lay gently on her skin. Water droplets from a recent storm hung on the leaves, catching the light like diamonds. All the frustrations of her journey were falling away, tipped out by wonderment at her surroundings.

Kirsten was no woofer. Hers was the only house which was separate and large enough for her to set up her research station. She'd come to an agreement with Ms Breeze that her house would be cleaned and serviced regularly. She would take her meals with the others in the main dining hall. Otherwise she would be left in peace to carry out her research.

She stopped in the middle of the track, paralysed by the sheer beauty of it all. To her left, vertiginous terraces tumbled down towards the river, buttressed by an immense cliff. She walked on. The main buildings seemed deserted. There was no sign of Ms Breeze or anyone else. She wondered where she might find her and why she hadn't been at the airport like she'd promised. The journey here had been a bit of a nightmare. It was a miracle that all her equipment had arrived intact. Landing at the airport just after eight in the morning, she'd had to do everything herself. She didn't blame the professor of zoology at the national university. He'd made it clear he would be at a conference in Brazil. Everything had been provided, from a Toyota Land Cruiser which she would have to return in a month's time down to the minutiae of her equipment and consumables. But where to find them and how to get to *Waters of Eostre* had been left to Ms Breeze and she hadn't turned up. No message, nothing. Kirsten had had to feel her way through customs and immigration, which had taken over an hour, pick up her car and then what? Her equipment was supposed to be in some warehouse on the outskirts of town and she had the address, but no one could tell her where that was without wanting to actually take her there, and she didn't feel comfortable with that. After driving over most of the potholes in Kumbala, she'd eventually got there to find that it was only ten minutes from the airport. The collection and loading of the equipment hadn't been a problem, but the journey to *Waters of Eostre* had. There was no satnav, and although she had a map, the road signs were totally inadequate. Most of those she'd asked didn't speak English. A journey which should have taken two and a half hours had taken four. It'd been fortunate that it had been daylight.

Anyhow here she was, and the place was utterly beautiful. Lush vegetation was casting lengthening shadows that slashed across each other like a painting by de Kooning. She estimated she had less than an hour before sunset. Which way to go? Ahead and to the left, the spectacular rock jutted out over the river. To her immediate right there seemed to be tangled jungle. Not now with so little time, although it would be fruitful territory for her work. Ahead and to the right she could glimpse cultivation and some interesting statues. She hadn't gone more than a few metres when she let out a gasp and darted forward. A chameleon lay clutching the branch of a coffee shrub. It was not quite perfectly camouflaged with the brown, grey, and green of its background. Kirsten identified it as an Elliott's Chameleon, not rare, but still exciting to find on her first afternoon. She approached it carefully, extending her left hand towards its head. It lunged round to the left with a breathy little roar and she grabbed it expertly with her right hand behind its neck. After studying its condition and sexing it as a male, she replaced it carefully on its branch. She noted her findings on her tablet and passed through a low arch into a garden of paradise.

Raised flowerbeds were laid out not in formal rows but in gentle curves softened still further by shrubs and trees. Water was everywhere: ponds, fountains, waterfalls, gullies, and streams. The sound of water gurgling, falling, and spraying was perfectly in tune with the birdsong which seemed to come from every corner of the garden. The hand of mankind had been laid perfectly upon nature, the cultivation sympathetic, with bold additions of pillars, carvings, and statues.

Kirsten was particularly drawn to a curving and diminishing line of marble columns which led the eye down to an exquisite pond with a wooden bridge, island, and miniature pagoda. On the far bank a life-like statue of a female figure in a sitting position seemed normal except that one of her legs had become detached from her body and was being held behind her neck. Eerily fascinated, Kirsten was admiring how the realism of the statue contrasted with the impossible position of that leg.

She jumped. A young man had appeared at her side. She'd been so preoccupied with the statue that she hadn't heard him coming.

'Hi, I'm Jake. You must be Kirsten, am I right?'

'Yes, hi, pleased to meet you.' She wasn't looking at him. 'That statue?'

He followed her gaze. 'What statue?'

For the first time Kirsten turned to stare at Jake. There wasn't another statue in sight.

'That one,' she pointed across the pond.

'That statue, hm, that statue. Ah yes, the one where the gaboon viper lives.'

Kirsten swung round to face him. 'Did you say gaboon viper? They're one of the most beautiful and venomous snakes in Africa. They're extremely rare and you say you've got one living here?'

'Oh yes, a whopper. At least three metres long, I'd say.'

'Do you see it often?' It sounded like a chat up line.

'Oh yes, all the time. Saw it earlier this afternoon, just by the statue. Expect it's there now.'

'Will you show it to me?'

'Me? Sorry, can't stand snakes. Give me the creeps, woo-hoo, wer-her. Got to run. See you at dinner.'

Kirsten crept slowly round the pond, her gaze fixed on the area at the base of the statue. Three metres? He must be exaggerating. The largest are normally less than two. Something else was wrong. Gaboon vipers live in dense woodland. It would be odd for one to be in open ground. Suddenly she realised she'd been fooled. He'd been having her on. She wasn't sure whether to be angry at her own gullibility - she was after all extremely tired - or whether to be pleased at the attention and that at least one person here had a sense of humour. Gaboon viper!'

'I'll be with you shortly.' For the second time in a few minutes, Kirsten jumped violently. The statue had spoken. Once more she stared at it, this time from twenty feet away. It hadn't moved. That leg really did look as though it had been detached and was being held behind its neck.

Din dumme idiot, it's Ms Breeze. She's been sitting there in a bronze-coloured leotard watching me all along. And that leg, it really is hers, that's one impressive contortion. Is she meditating? What am I meant to do, she thought angrily as she realised she'd been told to wait by the person who'd been supposed to meet her at the airport. She stood rooted, only able to take her eyes off Ms Breeze with difficulty. Slowly she stepped as though backing away from the gaboon viper itself before realising for the third time how stupid she'd been, and walking quickly back in the direction she'd come. She paused by a giant euphorbia tree. I must stop being jumpy, it's not like me.

Dusk had smothered the river far below and was beginning to sweep across the hillside. Soon the sun would set here too and the gardens would be in shade. It was still warm and the wonderful softness was like luxuriating in a bath. This was paradise.

She heard light footsteps coming up the path. 'You must be Kirsten. Tangle Breeze.' What a beautiful voice, like bells. 'I'm sorry I wasn't at the airport. It wasn't right.'

Kirsten, thinking she'd received an apology but an inadequate one, coolly returned Tangle's greeting.

'The moon last night had a distinct corona. Bad. One of the goats had an epileptic fit, which is not good in a full moon. Worse still, the stream over there started flowing in a way which worried me. When I investigated further, I found one of the men had been using a centrifugal pump higher up, filthy machine, which had disturbed the inward spiralling, gravitational pull of the water.'

What on earth is this woman on about, thought Kirsten. A pump upstream upsetting an inward spiralling, gravitational pull downstream? And for how long, for god's sake? She's talking scientific drivel.

'All these things happening within a few hours

of each other convinced me that the auspices weren't right for travel, so I stayed put.'

Thanks a bunch, thought Kirsten. What about my travel and auspices? And weren't the Breeze auspices right for making phone calls either?

'I hope you'll be happy here. Dinner's at seven, see you then.' Ms Breeze was already twenty metres away gliding towards the house.

Kirsten breathed in deeply, taking in the soft air and exhaling the last frustrations of the day. Suddenly she laughed. It was all too funny. She felt young, confident and very, very alive.

CHAPTER THREE

Tangle was showing new arrival Stanley around *Waters of Eostre*. Stanley had not enjoyed his flight. In his mid-fifties, he'd never been in an airplane before and hadn't known what to expect.

It'd started badly on the runway. Stanley's next-door neighbour, who hadn't ever flown either, had told him that air pressure could damage his eyes if he wore contact lenses. He'd been about to remove them when he heard an announcement to pay attention to the safety instructions. Rashly he attempted to concentrate on both, trying to eject a lens while keeping his other eye on the stewardess. With his hand cupped under his chin, it must have looked like he was blowing kisses at her. When told to check where his nearest exit was, Stanley, who had his head on one side, made the unwise decision to look behind him while still keeping an eye on the stewardess in front of him. Unable to complete this motion, he undid his seat belt, with the result that he pitched out into the aisle and the contact lens was lost. Now partly blind, Stanley clambered upright and stumbled back to his seat, head-butting a fellow passenger on the way.

By now the stewardess could do nothing to assist him, as she had to be seated for take-off. Just as the plane was about to surge forward, Stanley remembered that his specs were in his cabin bag in the overhead locker. He stood up and banged his head. He'd just managed to open the locker door as the engines started their wild crescendo. As the plane surged forward, Stanley hit his head again, this time more painfully on the corner of the open locker. Stanley and the plane roared down the runway, while high above the din there soared the soprano cries of the stewardess ordering him to sit down, sir.

Stanley struggled to get his bag down onto one knee. As the plane tilted into the air he just about managed to hang on. After more fumbling he found his spectacles. Unwisely, he tried to put them on before replacing the suitcase and returning to his seat. His newly restored vision meant that he could see movement through the window. As roofs of houses and cars flashed past, he was filled with nauseous vertigo. Half fainting, he staggered back and tripped over the foot of a passenger opposite. Spectacles, spectacle case, bag and Stanley all went in different directions.

After a minute or two groping seats, arms, legs and softer flesh which he couldn't see, Stanley broke down. He wanted his mother, who'd died last year, he wanted his wife, who'd left him, but the only source of female comfort was shouting at him down the aisle to sit down. There was nothing but air beneath him, he was heading far from home and still pointing skywards.

It took five minutes while the plane reached its cruising altitude, followed by another ten minutes of cooing from two stewardesses and a steward for Stanley's fellow passengers to be placated, but far longer for Stanley. His glasses were broken. Unsure of which was best, one contact lens or spectacles where one lens was missing and the other cracked, he spent the rest of the flight snivelling and winking at all around him.

Stanley had come to Zuzubia because six months earlier Tangle had added 'Anger Management' to the list of therapeutic benefits offered by *Waters of Eostre*. The Travel Supervising Officer at a South-London Borough Council had Googled 'Anger Management' and *Waters of Eostre* had appeared on his screen. A £2 million report following a case of fraud had concluded that decision-making at the council should be fragmented. As a result, several people were now involved in every activity, from building a community centre to ordering a paper clip. So it was that when the Therapy Treatment Officer had decided that Stanley should go on an Anger Management Course, she didn't know, wasn't allowed to know, what it would cost or where it was. Only the Travel Supervising Officer was allowed to know where it would be, but he wasn't allowed to know the cost either. So no one was in a position to question why Stanley's Anger Management Course was costing £26,000 and taking place in central Africa.

This place seemed so strange. Stanley ran his finger round under his collar. He was still wearing his sleeveless woollen sweater. But the birdsong was nice, though he wondered what might be lurking in the undergrowth. Snakes? Tarantulas? And how far did one have to go before one came across lions and tigers?

Stanley's attention was drifting as Tangle droned on. 'We employ six native workers. They live in a compound two miles away.' What a funny voice, very careful, saying each word exactly so. She must be a foreigner of some sort. 'We have a huge reverence for Nature here. We are her servants not her masters. We don't work the land, it commands us. The energy comes from the soil. It can move in one of two directions: spiralling inwards or spiralling outwards.'

Stanley yawned.

'Humans know about the hot, aggressive, outward-spiralling motion. It is very bad. Machines exploit that motion.' She gave a little grimace of disgust. 'This one's an outward-spiraller', she muttered, although Stanley failed to notice. 'We design all our tools to be inward-spiralling. They're planetary, centripetal.' Stanley wasn't the first new arrival at *Waters of Eostre* to wonder what on earth she was talking about. 'An increased concentration of qualigens enhances the levitational quality of the groundwater. This encourages growth and helps prevent the soil from drying out. Very important here in Zuzubia, where all the rains come at only one time of the year. Gravity originates from the atmosphere, levity from within the earth.' Stanley didn't know what gravity was, but he thought that levity meant something to be laughed at, so he laughed.

Tangle looked at him as someone might do who's not sure whether she's just heard a fart. 'Qualigens exist as an electrical potential in the water. Electricity is generated by the interaction of levitation and gravitation. You remember that Jacuzzi we saw up at the house earlier?'

Stanley didn't remember, simply because he didn't know what a Jacuzzi was.

'The bubbles in the Jacuzzi come from the qualigens in the water. Here, right here.' Stanley was looking the other way, appalled by a little African boy wearing no trousers and a top which was more holes than shirt. The boy was staring at him. Tangle had to pull him round. 'Do you know what this is?'

Stanley gazed at some rushes. 'It's a swamp.'

'No, beyond that, just above it. It's a tank. The sewage from the compost toilets is stored for eleven days before passing to its final stage in the reed bed, what you call a swamp. While it's in the tank it produces methane, from which bubbles rise, and those are the bubbles which pass through the water in the Jacuzzi.'

Most people expressed wonderment, some

shock. Tangle secretly liked either of those two reactions, but she hadn't liked a recently arrived Danish zoology graduate, who'd said, 'That's nonsense,' and had proceeded to give her some mathematical reason why the whole thing was impossible. Stanley, who didn't know what a compost toilet or a Jacuzzi was, said nothing.

Tangle soldiered on. 'The next duality, a crucial one, is that water, the living blood of a living Earth, can have masculine or feminine potential. If this aqueous fluid is created within the Earth, then the virgin water will develop a feminine, maternal, ovigenous potential. If it evolves in the atmosphere, then it will be endowed with a masculine or fertilising potential.' Tangle knew she was getting nowhere with Stanley, but habit and duty, which are forms of obstinacy, forced her to continue.

'The interface between the maternal Earth and the paternal atmosphere is the zone where the hymen can be caused to come into existence, allowing the productive marriage of these two influences. Can you guess how we achieve that relationship?' Tangle was so much on auto-pilot that she'd forgotten that Stanley wasn't going to answer that or any other question. She recalled with disgust how a month ago a newly arrived young man called Jake had responded, 'With slow and sensuous foreplay.' Ugh.

Tangle was getting nervous. If Stanley was prone to fits of anger, was one building up inside him now, ready to erupt? She wasn't worried about her own safety, but she didn't want her qualigens to be upset by outward-spiralling masculine potential.

Tangle needn't have worried. The cause of Stanley's anger was far away. He'd been cut off from the source of its fuel the moment he'd left England. His problem had started several years ago. Stanley and his then wife had become addicted to the BBC soap *Downsiders*. They'd loved the way the characters snarled, screamed and spat abuse at one another, so they started doing those things themselves. They relished it, realising as they entered middle age that they had found their true pleasure in life. They soon discovered that both the quantity and quality of these joys could be greatly increased if they widened their sphere of influence, so they abused those they met and were gratified when it produced a similar reaction in others. So whenever Stanley and his wife went shopping and someone's trolley was blocking the aisle, they would shove it with a loud 'tut' so that it crashed into the shelves or better still into the shopper's legs. And if they bumped into anyone in the street, an apology would be met with a 'For crying out loud.' Better still was when the result was a hostile retort and even, on one glorious occasion, a brief session of fisticuffs in the aisles of Tesco.

One evening, Stanley had watched big Kev on *Downsiders* getting his own back on young Ethan by shoulder-barging him off the pavement into the path of a van. This delighted Stanley so much that from now on he started initiating conflicts by deliberately bumping into people he merely didn't like the look of so that he could have the pleasure of saying 'For crying out loud' when they apologised. When Stanley and his wife had tired themselves out after a good day snarling and swearing at people, they sank back gratefully into their armchairs to watch their heroes and heroines of *Downsiders* doing the same and supplying them with new ways to improve their craft. And so they made a conscious effort next day to curl their lips a bit more, to improve on their use of sarcasm and remember to never, ever smile in public.

The knock-on effect was exhilarating. They detected, or imagined they detected, others doing the same, so that they could sense they were part of a nation-wide movement. They were right, as millions were fired up by *Downsiders* and, at a local level, by Stanley and his wife, to new levels of bitchiness. The ratings of *Downsiders* soared as more and more people tuned in to this fulfilling form of life, so that next day they could imagine themselves as the characters in *Downsiders*. Salt of the earth they are and so are we. Don't take no nonsense from no one. An eye for an eye, that's right.

The producers and script writers went for still more realism. They wanted Kev to knock Ellie about a bit, not that she didn't deserve it, mind. So he did. The viewers empathised immediately. Poor Kev, with the police and the landlord on his back, knocked Ellie about. Naughty Kev, the handsome villain, but we all love a bit of a rogue, don't we? And Ellie, poor Ellie, good for you Ellie, you give as good as you get, my darlin'.

Stanley and his wife responded immediately with enthusiasm. They too started knocking each other about a bit, just a little, and then tried it out on their cat, only when she deserved it, mind. It seemed natural, kind of right, now that they'd seen it done on the telly. Up and down the land other Stanleys and their wives took up the call and started boxing each other's ears like march hares. And the statistics proved it, they definitely proved it, that domestic violence was on the increase. And research showed it, it definitely showed it, that *Downsiders* was the programme most people felt mirrored their everyday lives. It didn't matter that Stanley and his wife knocked each other about, and their cat, because they were following what they'd seen on the telly. The BBC was proud of its programme, which was now winning awards. Giving the public what it wanted. Public service broadcasting. Kev knocked Ellie about because there were people like that in society. Everyone should be educated into knowing that this was so. How true to life, they said. Art reflecting reality. It wasn't, of course, it was the other way round, real people being corrupted by TV role models.

An independent survey revealed that soaps tended to show that villains succeeded. Audiences loved that, so the message being conveyed was that villainy paid. The results of the survey were suppressed.

It was Stanley's wife who caused his downfall. She'd been inspired, no, impassioned by Ellie, poor abused Ellie, who still managed to stick up for herself. 'Let me get at him,' Stanley's wife said to her friend Betty, expressing the desires of millions of women who hung nightly on Ellie's words and actions. 'I'll punch his lights out.' That confirmed it. Ellie was a no-nonsense person. Oh yes, she was the salt of the earth. Stanley's wife felt herself emboldened, empowered, legitimised. So when she forgot to put salt in the peas and Stanley slapped her one, she kneed him in the groin for all she was worth. Such an appropriate retaliation from a poor, defenceless woman. Unfortunately for her, in an earlier scene that evening, Kev of *Downsiders* had received a parking ticket from a female traffic warden. He'd told her where to stick it. In a later scene Kev had punched Wayne in a bar and sent him backwards through some swing doors. This was heroic stuff, and Stanley, still in agony from his wife's well-aimed knee, had conflated the two incidents in his mind: punching Wayne and being mistreated by a woman, the traffic warden. Stanley took a swing at his wife. Instead of reeling back through some swing doors (there weren't any), Stanley's wife stood there holding a broken jaw.

Stanley's wife confided in her friend Betty and told her it was a regular occurrence being punched by Stanley. It was happening all the time. Betty reported it to Social Services. Worse, Betty persuaded her that she should leave Stanley and move in with her, which she did. Stanley was in deep trouble, but escaped prosecution because the social worker persuaded the police that he could handle Stanley himself. The over-stretched police were only too happy to back off in order to improve their crime statistics and avoid having to fill in more paperwork. So Court was avoided; no charges, no gaol, no community service, no probation, not even a suspended sentence. What was in store for Stanley was a course in Anger Management.

All Tangle knew was that Stanley was the first woofer ever to have come to *Waters of Eostre* for Anger Management Therapy. She knew nothing of the causes nor the history behind it. Although she felt it her duty to help, if she could, she hadn't a clue how. If she'd been honest with herself, she would have admitted that the only reason why she'd added 'Anger Management' to her list of therapies was to attract money to *Waters of Eostre*. By far her biggest concern was that Stanley shouldn't have brought with him anything which might upset the equilibrium of her qualigens, bioflows and eco-rhythms.

Tangle knew she ought to end Stanley's induction tour for the time being, but she had yet to show him her pride and joy, and she couldn't resist pressing on. 'You've seen our toilets already and you know their results are composted. What I haven't yet shown you is the by-product.'

Stanley, not for the first time, wondered what she was on about. He did know what a by-product was, or thought he did. Somehow he couldn't get his mind away from sausages. But he wasn't going to proffer a guess. By now they'd re-entered the toilet block. Stanley was relieved that no one else seemed to be there. He was fearful of a practical demonstration.

Tangle opened one of the doors and beckoned

Stanley into a cubicle. He crept forward. She lifted a lid and invited him to peer down inside. He recoiled, feeling he was about to gag.

'It's quite odourless. There's a huge drop. The fall's important. Solid matter gathers pace as it falls and lands on the blades of a turbine, which generates electricity.'

Outside, Tangle got so excited that she'd failed to notice that she was back in full eco-speak. 'So many of us are attracted to nature-based spiritual traditions. Our eco-ethos is developing all the time. Science is the enemy of sustainable agriculture. It fails to listen to the land. Here it is the spiritual character of the land that we nurture. Principles of geomancy, *feng shui* and paganism apply. We create energetic harmony. Where *ch'i* collects in the landscape we release it through worship, ritual and prayer. These pillars, for instance' - Stanley had wondered what they were – 'are only there for one purpose: that the flow of the *ch'i* may curve around the brassicas.' They looked like cabbages to Stanley. He couldn't see any flow. And where was the cheese?

'Now this grove, for instance, has been created as a Nature Spirit Temple. It is a refuge for displaced spirits. Not all environmental energies are uplifting. Some may be stagnant or become an irritation. The spirits of place may be put out by building works. As for machinery, ugh!' Stanley felt quite sorry for Tangle. She seemed to be upset by unimportant things. 'To avoid this happening, we connect in meditation with them' - Stanley had forgotten who 'them' was - 'with a little ceremony of asking permission. We apologise for disruption about to be caused and ask for their blessing.

'Rocks form multiple functions. They store and release heat, but they also have esoteric properties provided they are treated with respect. They act as a wave guide to focus para-magnetism from the atmosphere into the soil by means of an acupuncturing effect. Now water, ah, don't get me onto water.' Stanley didn't think he was going to. The river was thankfully way below them, but there were those alarming toilets.

'Our pagan forbears knew all about the memory of water.' Tangle seemed to be reaching some sort of climax of ecstasy. 'Did you know that water can be polluted by hearing the mere mention of the name Hitler? But water is so responsive,' here Tangle gave a little girlish gasp of glee, 'that it responds instantly to love. We know this because over seventy percent of our bodies are water, and we can programme our own health with loving and healing thoughts.' Stanley wasn't into logic, but even he grasped that there was something a bit daft about this reasoning.

An African man came running up to them. He seemed to curtsey to Tangle. 'Excuse me, I have to go,' and she rushed up the slope towards the main housing block without telling Stanley what he was meant to do next. He'd just started moving off after her when a young man stepped out from behind some banana leaves.

'And after we've spouted garbage we always compost it. Hi, I'm Jake, you must be Stanley. Just arrived? People speak in many tongues here, but mostly New Age drivel. Tangle's very careful not to upset the stones, but she doesn't object to massacring the English language. Don't worry if you didn't understand anything. Most of it's nonsense, and some of the words she uses don't even exist. Are you here for the greens or the purification?'

'I'm here for...' Stanley checked himself. He'd only just held back the words 'Anger Management'. 'For the therapy.'

'Ah, the therapy. There's plenty of that here. Just be careful whose hands you hold. Most of them are out to steal your eco-flow, or is it your bioflow? I'd hug a rock if I were you, it's much safer. Well, I must get on, I've got a drain to dig. I think I'll try doing it just by thought processes. Upsets the displaced qualigens less. Anything you need? Pray.'

'There is something,' said Stanley nervously. This young man seemed as weird as the woman. 'Do you know where I can get new spectacles? And contact lenses?'

'That way, 130 miles. A day by road, a bit longer by river. Specs, that is. Contact lenses, probably not. Got to fly somewhere else for those. Must dash.'

So this is abroad, thought Stanley. It certainly seems foreign. He turned towards the houses and tripped over a rock. But no one was watching, and the rock didn't seem to mind.

CHAPTER FOUR

Mo Guterman, born Moshe in Cincinnati to German-Jewish parents, had been a rising star in TV production. His speciality and his passion had been Israeli-Palestinian relations. *Harmony*, a programme on Daniel Barenboim's West-Eastern Divan Orchestra, had been nominated for an award. His next project had been a documentary on the struggles of a Palestinian family in the face of Israeli settlement in the West Bank. An incensed Jewish lobby had threatened to withdraw funding from the station. 'Go on *America Tonight*, apologise, grovel, do what you have to', his boss had told him, 'but above all make it clear that you're going to do a programme on a struggling Israeli family desperate for accommodation, which you are, you bet your ass you are.'

Mo had done all that was asked, until the dying moments of the show. '*Evicted* was a huge mistake, I admit it,' he'd said with a sweet smile. 'I've learned my lesson. I realise there's no such thing as a balanced picture for those who've cornered the market in martyrdom.'

Powerful people, whose raw nerves had been twanged, made sure that Mo would never work in US TV production again. Still desperate to stay in television, he'd applied for an office job at the BBC in London and got it. A year later he'd gone freelance. He'd fallen in love with the UK, studied its history and its culture and become a wry observer of its people. His work permit had run out before he'd made it beyond production assistant. Unable to work in the USA or Britain, he'd managed to get himself onto a team filming crocodiles in Zuzubia. Working with Brits in London had been a pleasure, but this crew of unevolved apes was made up of public school chums who guffawed, slapped each other's backs and renewed their vows to each other by mocking those outside their clique. There was no subtlety. Their childish insults ranged from making sure that pork formed the main meal on Saturdays to calling their pet monkey Kike. Often Mo would enter the room to explosions of laughter as they peered at him from behind their hands. German jokes, oh how they loved their German jokes, were tweaked so that the Jews became central and Hitler was really rather a jolly good chap.

On a visit to Kumbala he'd gotten to hear about an organic farm and in desperation had contacted the owner, Tangwystl Breeze. She'd told him he'd be welcome as a woofer, so he'd walked out on his hooraying Henrys and made his way to *Waters of Eostre*. His brittle sensibility was shattered on his first night around the dinner table when he realised that a garrulous young Englishman, who clearly enjoyed mocking everything and everyone, was eyeing him up. Shit, they get everywhere, these goofies, why do I always have to end up living with them? He'd made up his mind that night. Gone would be the meek Jew turning the other cheek. Humility had been his great mistake on the film set. Now he would fight back, stand tall, walk proud and take no shit, like a true American.

Jake was delighted with the new arrival. Since he himself had only been at *Waters of Eostre* for a few months, he was flattered when Tangle had asked him to take Mo under his wing and show him the art of permaculture. Mo soon realised that he couldn't believe a word he was told. Jake had tried to convince him that Tangle was a witch and yes, she did look a bit like that, but an extremely attractive one.

'Apply liquid fertiliser only in the evenings, otherwise it evaporates. Always mix it fresh. Put a little water in the can, then add the fertiliser, stirring vigorously. Fill the can to the top with more water and stir again.' That sounded reasonable.

'Now for the mix. We use root of hemlock as the base, but it has to be dug in the dark. Tangle's very specific about that. Cool it with a baboon's blood and then add liver of a blaspheming Jew... sorry.' Jake looked genuinely shamefaced, but Mo was seething. This was like being back on the film set.

'Gall of a goat and slips of yew slivered in the moon's eclipse. Fillet of a fenny snake.'

'Macbeth, you motherfucker! It's the witches in Macbeth.'

'You know Macbeth? I didn't know you had Shakespeare in America. Silly me, of course you do, the sanitised Disney version with the feel-good ending.'

Whatever the stronger version of slighted was, Mo felt it. 'Now you just wait one minute here. Don't you go playing the superior with me. Our culture dominates yours.'

'Oh excuse me so it does, by appealing to the lowest common denominator. A nation that takes all the subtlety out of Winnie the Pooh has little trouble with Shakespeare. Take a good story, rinse out all sense of irony, add spoonfuls of sugar and make sure everyone goes home with a happy ending. If there's any history, rewrite it, making sure of course that the heroes are all American and that they win. What was it someone said about Hollywood? Hollywood is an overpowering giant who, when he opens his mouth to talk, talks baby talk.'

Mo's blood was rising. He was still smarting from the Lord Snooties he'd just left. 'You sneer at my culture, do you? But the trouble with you limeys, you keep gorging yourselves on it. What's your second national anthem? *There'll be Blue Birds over the White Cliffs of Dover*. An American wrote that. I've lived long enough in England to know there aren't any blue birds there. The guy who wrote it in the States assumed that there were. Yet still you lapped it up. You should have gotten Vera Lynn to sing about blue tits. That would have been more appropriate in every sense.'

If Jake was impressed, he didn't let on. 'You're right, we should never underestimate the power of the USA. The combination of money, bad taste and certainty is irresistible. But a lot of what you do comes from insecurity. It has to be American this and American that, *American Dreamz, American Werewolf in London;* the number of movies produced by Hollywood with American in the title runs to hundreds. Your war films have to have US heroes even when it was an all-British event. In the movie *U-571* it's Americans who crack the Nazi code. You even pinch our titles. Where does *The Thin Red Line* come from? It was the heroic Sutherland Highlanders at the battle of Balaklava.'

'At least we stand up for ourselves. You English are a race of quitters. It's instilled in you from childhood. Take your railway engine books. You mock and despise Gordon the Big Engine while you root instead for pathetic, tootling little Thomas the Tank Engine. That's why you're shunting down the branch line of world influence. You love losing. You'd rather remember an inglorious defeat than a glorious victory. You mentioned Balaklava just now? You English won the battle, but all you remember is the bit that went wrong, the Charge of the Light Brigade.'

This bloke's just the sort of sparring partner I want, thought Jake. He knows his Britain and he knows his history. Right, let's try a new tack. 'You take your heroes to extremes. Rambo, our royalty,

God and Superman, they're all so perfect it's a wonder you can tell them apart.'

'At least we know who our heroes are. Admit it, you can't get enough of the USA. A hurricane can cause hundreds of deaths in Cuba or Haiti and the BBC hardly mentions it, but once it gets to the American coast your news carries photos of bent lamp posts and stacked sand bags. You've got a large Asian population who, back home in places like Bangladesh, drown in their thousands whenever the Ganges-Brahmaputra delta floods. What do they think when they get ignored in favour of, shock-horror, a few people who've been flooded out of their homes in Louisiana? Your children are steeped in our culture from infancy. On Sunday mornings, while their parents are in bed with their hangovers, your kids are in front of their TVs watching, what? American cartoons, American schmaltz, and American action. When it comes to culture, we've got you by the twisty whiskers. Ask your adolescents about their civil war. Ninety percent won't understand the question and the other ten percent will think it was fought between Confederates and Yankees.'

Jake was well into his stride now. 'You think you're doing the world a favour with your war on terror. You use drones to kill innocent people and then are outraged when your outgunned opponents don't play by your rules. Remember that moment in the Bond Movie when Roger Moore is forced to fight with a martial arts champion? Obviously he's at a huge disadvantage, so what does he do? While his opponent is going through the elaborate opening ritual, Bond gives him one, jumps up and runs off. Nice one, James.'

Not much work was being done while all this was going on. Suddenly Jake remembered he was meant to be teaching Mo permaculture. 'See these yam saplings here, something's been eating them. Look, see here? Little worms.'

'Right, I'll run and get the DDT.'

Jake smiled with delight at Mo's sarcasm. 'Trouble is the rains are early this year.'

'Global warming?'

'You, an American, believe in global warning?'

'Of course not, it's bad news, and we don't believe in bad news, right?'

'Mm.' Jake sounded appreciative. 'Irony, eh?'

'Well, it's better than what you serve up. All you teach your kids is that smutty sense of humour of which you're so proud.' Mo had the Hooray Henrys fully in his vision. 'Mr Jeremy Fisher all slippy-sloppy in his back passage, tee-hee-hee, adjusting his tackle. Then he starts jerking on his rod, hee-haw. As for Timmy Willie, now there's a name, sitting there cracking his nuts, or is that Squirrel Nutkin? Then there's Mr McGregor in his potting shed, pricking out...'

Jake could hold it in no longer. He exploded with laughter. Mo looked at him with surprise. He'd meant to hit this English bastard, not tickle him.

'Christ, here comes Tangle, look busy.' Jake just managed to pick up a rake in time. Tangle paused only briefly, smiling slightly, giving Jake's heart the wobbles. She glided on down the path to an assignment with some force of nature.

Jake was following her with dreamy eyes.

'Hey, *luftmensh,* look at you! I do believe you fancy her.'

Slowly Jake loosened his gaze and turned to his companion. 'As if you didn't. Where was I?'

'Lustily dreaming of the unattainable? I think you were loosing off with your pop-gun at all things American.'

'Ah yes. And there's your politics. Every four years the American people sit in front of their screens trying to decide which candidate has spent the most money on buying the result. What they don't realise is that the decision's already been made for them, because they're suckers for the billions of dollars spent on political advertising paid for by lobbyists and big business, big oil, big pharma, who buy the candidates and dictate their policies. In most countries that would be called corruption.'

'And how about you? You have a special form of corruption tailor-made for you Snooties.' Again, an image of the Bullingdon Henrys was before Mo. 'It's called the Honours System. Your Prime Minister is embarrassed by a scandal. How does he get out of it? Simple, he appoints Sir Pratt Bogey to head a public enquiry, because Sir Pratt Bogey is a safe pair of hands, and the reason for that is that Sir Pratt Bogey is waiting for his peerage, so he delivers a bland report exonerating the Prime Minister and his government, with a few minor criticisms to throw the public off the scent. The Prime Minister waits for a decent length of time, and then Sir Pratt Bogey steps into his ermine. And so it goes on down the line.'

'Public enquiries?'

'No, you *putz,* favours right down to the lowest form of gong, what do you call them?'

'MBEs, no maybe OBEs, I don't know or care.'

'Whatever. Jerks put forward by their sponsors in return for favours. When newly elevated Dame Kiss Myass, who's kissed everyone else's, kneels before the Queen, Lizzie should shout out 'For services to your Sponsors. Here comes Tangle again. Mm, I do see what you mean.'

CHAPTER FIVE

Kirsten leapt back holding her finger. A small dome of blood was forming rapidly over the wound. The fire skink she'd been stalking had vanished. She knew they had a painful bite, but she didn't think she'd got close enough for that.

Joseph arrived by her side. 'Let me look at it.' She'd become more and more impressed with her African assistant. He didn't have specialist knowledge of reptiles and amphibians, but his bush craft was sound and he was dedicated, keen to learn and quietly efficient. 'May I see your finger?' It was beginning to throb.

Without warning, he seized her wrist, bent down and sank his teeth on either side of the wound. She let out a cry, but his grip was strong. By the time she realised he was sucking on her blood, he'd turned away and spat ferociously, before repeating the process several times. He finally released her.

'I am sorry that I had to do that,' he said quietly

but far from humbly. The poison of the *mwanajeshi* is bad if you do not treat it quickly. You must see a doctor. I will drive you.'

'But the skink?'

'It was not the skink. You were not close enough, look.' He showed her the vicious thorns of a small bush where her hand had been a couple of minutes earlier. 'We call it *mwanajeshi,* the soldier. Come, we should go now.'

The pulsating pain had started to ease on the long drive to the hospital, replaced by a steady ache spreading up her arm. Anxiety and shock were numbing out thought, but even so she realised how lucky she was to have this considerate and intelligent man by her side.

'This evening we have a visitor.' To Jake, Tangle's voice sounded flat. She could be effusive, fey, even occasionally assertive, but never flat. She was usually too Welshly musical for that. There was a tension about her tonight. Either she was upset or something was up. He watched her closely. He didn't know what it was, but he was intrigued.

Outside on the veranda, moths flew around a lamp in dancing clouds to a deafening background of chirruping and screeching of crickets and frogs. Shutters let through the night air, at least for now, but not the insects, which presented their undersides as they swarmed over the mesh. A flesh-coloured gecko, which appeared every night in the rafters, peered down at the diners.

Tangle fingered her black mane in a way which appeared both nervous and seductive. 'Kirsten has had a small accident, a poisonous thorn. She's all right. She's on her way back from the hospital now.' She kept glancing at her visitor, a suave Englishman in his fifties. He had swept back hair and wore a beige tropical suit.

'This is Mr Garston Peters. Mr Peters has a proposition which, erm, well, he thinks, he'd like you to hear.' An odd choice of words, thought Mo. Does that mean that Tangle wouldn't like us to hear it?

'Honoured to be here.' He sounds as sincere as a politician praising a baby a week before polling day, thought Jake, whose rebelliousness had been roused. He'd taken instant exception to the obsequiousness of Tangle calling him Mr Peters.

'May I suggest,' Peters turned to Tangle on his left, 'that we enjoy our meal, which I'm sure will be as superb as ever, and then I'll say a few words and take questions at the end.'

They all started eating. No one spoke. Distant thunder was muttering somewhere along the river. Tangle seemed to be chasing salad leaves around her plate. Every now and then she stopped and looked up in exasperation, as though unable to focus on anything. She would have been flabbergasted had she known that Mo, so newly arrived, actually knew quite a lot about Mr Garston Peters.

Kirsten entered silently. Tangle didn't seem to notice, and when she did, she sat up sharply, dropping her knife with a clatter. 'How are you feeling?'

Kirsten held a bandaged finger aloft and smiled wanly. Stanley's eyes followed to where she seemed to be pointing, vaguely in the direction of the lizard. No one else was looking up there. Stanley didn't really understand who Kirsten was. She didn't seem to do any work, and she was always going on about frogs and snakes and things.

Peters leaned back in his chair. 'Ah, you must be Kirsten. I've heard so much about you. I'm Garston Peters, perhaps we can have a chat afterwards. I'd love to hear what you've been up to.' Mo thought that sounded rather threatening. Kirsten, who was halfway across the room, paused and stared hard at Peters. Then she quietly took her place at the table, relieved that she didn't have to explain anything now. It'd been a frustrating day, and she was starving. Unknown to the rest of them, Kirsten too knew something about Garston Peters.

Jake had planned to bolt down his food and then break the monastic silence which had followed Kirsten's entrance. But he'd noticed something odd. Tangle, as usual, was nibbling at her vegan rabbit food. The rest of them were struggling with some rather nondescript meat which he suspected might be goat. But their guest had been served two plump birds like partridges or quails. Jake leaned rudely over Peters' plate, shaking his head rapidly as though trying to sprinkle dandruff. 'The rains have come early.' He screwed his head round and looked up into Peters' face. 'I hope the weather isn't turning *fowl*.' Then he withdrew his head and turned to Kirsten. 'When you were at the hospital today, did you receive *special treatment*?' She gave him a pitying look.

They all finished eating in silence. Peters, who hadn't acknowledged anything Jake had said or done, picked up a knife and tapped his wine glass as though he were about to address an audience of fifty rather than five. 'Ahem,' said Jake rudely.

'I'm sure we're all grateful for a splendid meal.' He beamed at Tangle, who unsuccessfully tried to force a smile. 'I thought you'd all be interested to know that I have an exciting new venture for *Waters of Eostre*. Jake shook his shoulders up and down, grinning in mock excitement. Mo looked suspicious, Kirsten wary. Stanley wondered what adventure this man had in store.

'I've discovered an amazing African lady who lives not far from here. She's a superb cook and her sauces have to be tasted to be believed.'

'Never reveal your sauces,' interrupted Jake.

This time Peters shot him a look of disgust. 'Now, I've managed to get Mama Kuli, that's her name, to disclose the recipes. I'm going to manufacture and market them, Mama Kuli's whatever-it-happens-to-be sauce.' He surveyed his audience, looking for an enthusiastic response, and got none. Tangle was staring at her lap, Jake was cocking an eyebrow cheekily and the others were looking hostile or bored. 'Now it's important that we can claim that the ingredients are organic, and that's where you come in, Tangwystl.'

Jake spluttered, only just managing to return his coffee cup to its saucer without breaking it. I could have done that, I could have called her

Tangwystl, I still can. He stared at her. She was wearing a long salmon pink evening gown. Her black hair twisted around her neck and fell between her breasts. Her face is lined, her eyes close together and hawkish, she has a pointy chin, she's nearly twice my age, what am I thinking, but what the hell. 'Wow,' he said out loud, making Tangle look up at him and then sharply lower her eyes. Jake suddenly realised that everyone was staring at him except Tangle, whose blush was delightfully matching her dress.

'Sorry.' Jake smirked. He didn't look it, he looked triumphant.

Peters continued, 'As I was saying, I've talked to Tangwystl, and I'm firmly of the opinion that it will be possible to produce most of the raw ingredients here. It will be hard work.' He sounded severe. 'We intend to get product to market within twenty months, and we will have to bring in more African labour. But it's an exciting opportunity, and I want to make sure that you guys are behind it. What do you think?'

Jake was about to ask what was in it for them, but Mo's question lashed through the air like a whip. 'What's in it for Mama Kuli?'

Peters laughed affably. 'Oh, you needn't worry about her. She won't be interested in what we're doing. All she wants is to continue making sauces for her family.'

'It's her recipe.' There was no smile on Mo's face, and no softening charm. 'What royalty will you be paying her?'

'Don't you worry about her. She won't be any

worse off. Her sauces wouldn't be going anywhere if it weren't for me.'

Jake lacked Mo's gravitas. 'And your sauces wouldn't be going anywhere if it wasn't for her.'

Garston rounded on him. 'Know this, young man, I've been in this country a long time, long enough to know that its economy is nothing without people like me to develop its exports.'

Jake was rising in his chair, but Mo put a restraining hand on his arm. 'I hear you've got a stake in the new water plant at Ngombe?' His voice was as icy as his stare. 'Is it true that the initial feasibility study cost 1.8 million US dollars?'

'Something like that.' Peters gave a dismissive flick of his head.

'And that over half a million bucks of that went on PR consultants to promote privatisation?'

'Oh, I dare say. Look, you're not suggesting that we should have gone ahead without a feasibility study, are you?'

Tangle, Jake and Kirsten were staring at Mo, wondering how he knew all this. Stanley, who was still on Mama Kuli's sauces, wondered why she should get a Royalty. Was she about to become some sort of tribal queen?

'Mr Peters, are you also aware that a study by UNESCO last year concluded that developing countries should not privatise their water systems, the reason being that foreign companies siphon off around eighty percent of the development budget and ninety percent of the income?'

'You're speaking to the wrong person,' Peters

snapped, all trace of affability gone. 'The Government of Zuzubia made the decision, not me.'

Mo had read that most of the cabinet had vast overseas bank accounts and it was obvious where their money came from. But he wasn't foolish enough to say so, or he'd be on a plane within forty-eight hours. How did he know? Because prior to coming out to film crocodiles, he'd researched the economic and political scene in Zuzubia and had been appalled at what he'd uncovered.

———

Kirsten was beginning to dread her private chat with Peters after the meal. She was thinking of Joseph and what he'd told her on the drive back from hospital. Curious to know more about him, she'd asked about his village.

'My village no longer has water. We now have to walk four miles each way to get it from a well. It is hard.'

'But the rains have come early this year. Surely there's enough water, or soon will be?'

'It is not the rains. It is the golf course. They drained the land to make a golf course. There was a well a mile away, but they have taken that for their own water. In the dry season, the land is brown, but the golf course it is green from all the water which they spray onto it. Our water.'

'That is terrible, Joseph. Who is doing it?'

The Minister of Finance, Godson Malembe, he is a bad man. He is paid by a company called

Enlandia, which has done a deal with a big overseas company.'

'Is there no publicity? Has there been no international outcry?'

'The newspapers here are all controlled by Mr Malembe. I do not know of any international outcry. I do not think so. But you have not heard the worst. My own village has been lucky. Although we have to walk far to get water, we have been allowed to stay. A hundred and thirty people in a village where the golf course has been built were taken from their homes and moved to a place forty miles away. There is no water there at all, not even if they walk far.' He sounded depressed rather than angry.

'There are notices all around the edge of the golf course. They tell the people inside, do not go beyond here, it is dangerous, you will be leaving the area protected by the guards. It has never been dangerous, it is these people who say that it is dangerous, they make it so. They make suspicion and mistrust. On the back of these notices it says only members are allowed beyond here. That is what it says to people who have lived there all their lives, whose ancestors are buried there. The notices, they say you are no longer allowed on your own land. They say that to be a member of the golf course costs over six thousand dollars a year. Top people in the government are, how do you say it, free members?'

'Honorary members.' Kirsten was familiar with the term from her health club in England.

'Honorary members. But when a local businessman, a Zuzubian, a good man respected by the people, tried to become a member, they turned him away.'

'That's racism. That's apartheid.'

'That is Zuzubia!' For the first time, Joseph raised his voice.

'That company here, what did you say its name was?'

'Enlandia. It is run by a man called Garston Peters. He sometimes comes to *Waters of Eostre*.'

Kirsten was fairly sure she hadn't seen him. Her mind was racing, but she was pulled up with a jerk when Joseph said, 'He has a relationship with Miss Breeze.'

'A relationship? You mean... What do you mean?'

'I do not know.' Joseph looked sullen, which was unlike him.

'Joseph, I must know. Please won't you tell me? Are you saying they are lovers?'

He looked at her sharply, then turned back to the road. 'No, I am not saying that.'

'Then what?'

'Miss Breeze is a good lady. I do not believe that she would do anything bad. Mr Peters is a powerful man. It is not easy to say no to him. When Mr Peters speaks, people are forced to listen.'

'And what if they don't?'

'Then life will be hard for them. Mr Peters could make it difficult for Miss Breeze to sell what she grows. I think maybe it is that.' Joseph stared solidly ahead at the road, his tight expression making it quite clear that he had no intention of saying anything else on the matter.

Mo's intervention had stunned everyone. Kirsten was trying to think fast. Should she pitch in now in support of Mo, using what Joseph had told her this afternoon? She wasn't a coward, but she needed to be careful. Joseph was her only assistant. It wouldn't take Peters long to find out where her information had come from. She decided to bide her time and confide in Mo later.

Peters had reacted to Mo's attack by standing up. He turned towards Tangle. 'A word with you in private.'

'Look, Boyo, don't you think we've got a right to hear it too?' Jake's attempt at a Welsh accent sounded more like an Indian's. Again Mo put a restraining hand on his shoulder. Peters and Tangle left the room in silence. The moment the door closed behind them, Kirsten was at Mo's side.

'There's something you should know, if you don't already.' She was talking quietly and rapidly, leaning into his ear. He sat there nodding, receiving all she'd heard from Joseph. At the end, he simply murmured, '*Oy Gutt.*'

In Tangle's office, Peters swung round to face her. 'I told you to employ types who only want to grow things and won't go poking around. Where did you get him from?'

Tangle was slow to answer, not because she was frightened, though she was, but because her yoga training told her to control her breathing first. 'Mo approached me. He was already out here.'

'What about the others? That Jake, he seems like a punk. Juvenile but harmless?'

'That about sums him up. He's a good worker, though.'

'That mossback, what's his name, Stanley?'

'Lacking up top. He's totally innocuous. Give him something to do and he does it. Get him to think for himself and I'm wasting my time.'

'Good. And the girl?'

'She's the one who's over in the big house. She's not part of my team.'

'Yes, I know that, the research worker. Has she been any trouble? Been asking any awkward questions?'

'No, she just seems to get on with her work.'

'What about your African workers? How many have you got now?'

'Six.'

'Any problems? Any of them showing signs of getting above their station?'

'None at all.'

'Look, Tangwystl, you're going to have to control that smart arse Guterman. Either that or get rid of him.'

'That is my affair, not yours.' She spoke slowly and carefully, hearing herself speak as though it were someone else.

Peters stared at her, unused to anything but submission. He could tell that she was holding his gaze with difficulty. 'I came here to help you grow your whimsical plaything into something worthwhile. If you wish to remain footling around with your statues and witchcraft, that's up to you. But you may find that the market for your produce has become, shall we say, difficult. Since what you seem to be cultivating is a hotbed of dissent...' He started to walk away, then spun round to face her. 'You need to put your house in order. You are responsible for everyone and everything here. If you insist on operating in a bubble of isolation, you might find your position an extremely lonely one.' With that he left the room.

She listened to his car start up and fade into the night. She'd surprised herself as much as him. She stood breathing rapidly. Then she smiled to herself. After all, the moon is in her last quarter, and today is an auspicious *tithi.* Garston's *nakshatra* is *Ashlesha,* well that figures. So, Garston Peters, I'm a *Magha,* so you'd better watch out.

She slipped quietly back into the room, fearful of her reception. Kirsten was smiling at her. Mo stood up and led her gently by the arm to her seat. She burst into tears. Jake's heart started beating rapidly. Stanley was blinking.

CHAPTER SIX

Eight miles to the east of *Waters of Eostre, Crowned Crane Lodge* was a very different kind of establishment. Spread along the north bank of the river, it was well within the game park. The opulent dining room overhung the water so that guests could peer into the eyes of hippos and crocodiles only a few metres away. No ethos of qualigens or woofers here. When the water eddied in the current, as it was doing now due to the unseasonal rain, no one cared a damn whether its spiral was inward or outward. What defined *Crowned Crane Lodge* was unrestrained luxury, attention to detail and an exclusivity which demanded just one thing: that guests should pay the room rate of 26,000 dollars a week.

Dinner over, a group of three new arrivals were sitting round the fire. Although it had rained all day, the sky had now cleared. At the press of a button, a huge mechanical awning had swung back to reveal the night sky. Ultrasound anti-mosquito machines had slid silently into place around the guests, who were enjoying watching the sparks from a brazier spiral up towards the stars. Distant lightning played on the horizon to the east. Near at hand, grunts and snorts from goodness knows what animals out there provided an exotic background.

Teeny Trumper was only ever short of words in the presence of her husband, Chest. Back home in her Long Island mansion, Teeny was the queen of her socialite circle. She liked to portray herself as a promoter of good causes, but what the whole of her circle knew was that the coffee was more important than the causes, and the gossip was more important than the coffee.

Teeny's husband Chest, a film producer with the physique of an ox and a bellow to match, was not one to wait to be asked what had brought him to Zuzubia.

'I'm here for just two things: to get ideas for an African movie I'm going to make. There hasn't been what you might call a real African epic since *Mogambo* in '53. What a movie that was; Gable, Kelly, Gardner, they say they don't make 'em like that no more, well, depends on who you mean by 'they'. We'll see. And the other thing I want to do is bag some of the biggest trophies since Hemingway.'

'I think you'll find that rather hard.' The voice belonged to a tall, grey-haired Englishman in an immaculate pale blue safari suit and gold cravat. 'There's only a fraction of the game left from Hemingway's day. The best specimens were bagged, as you put it, by poachers long ago.'

Granville Summers was a retired surgeon. Like

many medical consultants, he'd considered himself to be God. To most of the hospital staff he'd merely been a remote but dangerous being who, although powerful, behaved rather badly like a deity feared by ancient Romans. His private patients, on the other hand, would fondly remember Mr Summers' suave and sympathetic manner, the calm efficiency of his crisp-suited PA, the aromatic smell of coffee in the waiting room, the lovely fragrance of gardenias, and the attentive way they were ushered into the impressive room of his large house with its expensive furniture and oil paintings. 'Was that Fragonard really an original?' Indeed it was, Mr Summers had confirmed. Private patients were always seen promptly, diagnosed and, if necessary, operated on without delay, regardless of the seriousness of their condition. And every time this happened, NHS patients in the queue would receive a letter which started 'I regret to inform you that, due to unforeseen circumstances...' No one thought about the irony of the word 'unforeseen'. Private patients were foreseen - seen before - the plebs who were forced to depend solely on the NHS for their health and survival.

Granville Summers had long forgotten about Derek Fuller. He didn't recall his name, his face nor the organ which passed too late through his hands. It may seem strange not to remember someone you've killed, but Granville Summers had killed many men, women and children, and considered himself too professional to worry about it. Compliant and very British Mr Fuller, a plumber's mate by trade, had accepted without question that, due to unforeseen circumstances, his life-saving operation had had to be postponed three times in four months. He'd assumed that the operating theatre and Mr Summers were having to deal with emergency cases even more urgent than his own. It must be the same for everyone, just got to live with it, a fact of life. In reality it was a fact of death, and Mr Fuller would just have to die with it.

But we mustn't point the finger at Granville Summers. It was the System, whereby consultants were allowed to use NHS facilities while giving priority to their private patients, pocketing huge sums of money from both their patients and the tax payer. Neither *The Guardian* (much) nor the *Daily Mail* (at all) questioned the System, not the fundamental parts, because these things had been going on for a long time, before 1947 when the NHS was created, a time when the rich and privileged were expected to have rights over the poor and vulnerable. No one individual was to blame, therefore no one was, and anyhow Granville Summers had retired. But eighty-nine-year-old Mrs Dittup spending fourteen hours on a trolley in a hospital corridor, now that was News, because it didn't happen very often, even though the *Daily Mail* pretended it did.

Of course neither Chest Trumper nor his wife Teeny knew any of this, and would not have been interested in any case, being wealthy and from a country where it was expected that the rich should have greater rights than the poor when it came to health, life and death. All Chest knew was that this high hat sitting opposite him had dared to question one of the reasons for his being here, to bag some of the biggest trophies since Hemingway. But for now he wanted to concentrate on his even greater love, making movies.

'I'm looking for a hero who transformed Africa.'

'Livingstone?' Granville doubted the suitability of his suggestion, guessing correctly that Chest's definition of the word hero was extremely narrow.

'Who's he?'

'He was an explorer who opened up the heart of Africa.'

'What type of gun did he carry?'

'He didn't, he was a missionary.'

'No good then. Who else?'

'You could try Richard Burton and John Hanning Speke. They went out to discover the source of the Nile and hated each other's guts.'

'Burton you say? Did they fight over Liz Taylor? You could be onto something there.'

Granville felt he was getting to know his man. 'Not the same chap. A hundred years earlier.'

Chest was brilliant at his job. His ignorance of history and the world outside the USA was spectacular. This was entirely appropriate, as it reflected those who watched his films. The accuracy of history was an irrelevance to Chest, who knew his movie-going public. But he had to start somewhere, and this smooth-assed limey seemed to know his way-back-whens.

Granville looked at him thoughtfully. 'I think I may have your man, a maverick who defied his government, a committed Christian who held out heroically against the massed hordes of Muslim

Dervishes. Heavily outnumbered, he faced them alone on the steps of his palace in Khartoum.'

Chest slammed his whisky glass down hard onto the table. 'That sounds more like it. Who is this fella?'

'General Gordon.'

'Gordy, like the name.'

'Gordon.'

'Sounds kinda Flashy, get it?' He grinned at Teeny who showed that she did and at Granville, who pretended he didn't. 'Just what the punters like.'

Some animal across the river let out a ferocious roar. Teeny looked round nervously, but the two men ignored it.

'What was the other name you mentioned?'

'Khartoum. That was the place where he died.'

'Car Tomb. I like it. Has a kinda ring to it. Where did you say it was?'

'I didn't. It's in the desert on the banks of the Nile, well over a thousand miles north of here.'

'In the desert. Car Tomb. Yes, that's it. I see baking heat and twisted metal, camels and pyramids.'

'The pyramids aren't anywhere near there.'

'Then we'll move them.'

'I don't think you can do that, Sweetie.' Teeny was always on hand to rein in Chest's wilder fantasies. 'I don't think the authorities in Vegas would let you.'

'Quite right, my Baby Cake, quite right. We'll forget that one. We'll build some pyramids of our own in Car Tomb. But wait one minute. You say Gordy died there. How did he die?'

'He was hacked to pieces by a mob of Dervishes on the steps of the palace. He faced them alone.'

'Hm. Not a good ending. Not what the great American public wants. It's gotta end good.'

'Well it didn't for him,' said Granville somewhat irritably. 'But he was avenged.'

'Ah now, that's better. Go on.'

'General Kitchener came up the Nile with a vast army and defeated the Dervishes at the Battle of Omdurman.'

'Kitchener? No, he won't do, sounds like a domestic.'

'Omdurman was the last great cavalry charge in history.'

'Oh dear me no,' Chest chuckled, 'you've got that one wrong, it was in *The Crusades*.'

Again, Granville was irritated. Could this idiot really think that a battle in the middle of Africa was older than the Crusades? 'It was Omdurman in 1898,' he said stiffly.

'*The Crusades,* Cecil B DeMille 1935. That's way after yours. See? Never catch me out on the movies. Know them all.'

Granville threw up his hands in a gesture of despair. Chest ignored him. Teeny, sensing the tension, cooed, 'Go on dearest.'

'Maybe we should switch these dudes, have Gordy riding in to save Kitchen Boy.'

'Kitchener. *Your Country Needs You*.'

'So right, pal, and it's gonna get me. Where was I?'

'Kitchener.'

'Yea, him, snivelling little chicken liver. Say, I forgot to ask, who were these guys, I mean what nationality?'

'Both British.' Granville looked at him severely.

'Well, Kitchener can be a Brit, that's fine, but I think we'd better have Gordy an American.'

'It's Gordon.'

'You think so?'

'It's his name.' Granville's stare was as cold as his voice.

'Don't mean a thing. Who cares about Buffalo Bill's and the Sundance Kid's real names? Look, you've been a great help giving me all this information.' Chest held up a hand. 'No, really, I mean it. But never forget that a movie exists to entertain, that and to make the punters go home feeling good. That's the beginning and end of it. "Pictures are for entertainment; messages should be sent via Western Union." The great Sam Goldwyn said that. Here's another great quotation. "All history is bunk." '

'Henry Ford.'

'Very good, Granville. Pleased to meet you by the way, you're a great guy. There's just two things wrong with history. Know what they are?'

Granville looked warily at him.

'H and I. Take out those two letters and what are you left with? The story! That's all that matters, the story. So you see, Granville, I can have Gordy fighting on top of the pyramids and taking off in a helicopter and flying into the sunset to live happily ever after if that's what the public's gonna like. Now, who else was a big shot in the desert?'

'Tutankhamun, Ramses, Nefertiti.'

'Interesting names, Granville. No, I mean it. Now, one at a time slowly if you will.'

'Tutankhamun was a boy king.'

'That's ok. Tootin' Car Moon would sound a bit wet on a hunkin' great fella, but a boy might just pull it off. We'll have him. Next?'

'Ramses.'

'Like it. Kinda follows on from Rambo. Who's the last guy?'

'Nefertiti, a queen.'

'A pansy? A left-handed mintie? A limp wrist? Well, I don't know about that. It might go down on the East and West Coasts, but I've got the South to consider...'

'A woman.'

'A chick, hey? Nef-er-titi. Nope, I don't think we can have that one. Even if the American public were to put up with titis on screen, the censors sure wouldn't.' He shook his head, as though clearing some troublesome insect. 'Now for the action. The action, Granville, that's what the public comes for. For the Car Tomb there's gotta be a chase; we'll make it a good one, with a wreck. The other thing we've gotta have is a grand shoot-out. Let me see, something along the lines of, I've got it, how the Colt 45 conquered Africa.'

'But it didn't.'

'Granville, Granville, no of course it didn't, you and I know that.' Granville wasn't sure that Chest really did. 'Not everyone will believe it and a few critics will carp as they always do, but the majority will go for it. The numbers game, Granville; think box office, butts on seats. If Hollywood says it happened, then for most of the movie-going public it did. So Colt 45 it is. Now, we need someone who can draw.'

'You mean an artist.'

'Yea, someone who does it real good. Come on, Granville, who was the greatest drawer in history?'

'Leonardo?'

'Leonardo. Who's he?'

'Da Vinci?'

'Nope, never heard of him. Describe him.'

'He was an Italian painter in the late fifteenth and early sixteenth centuries.'

Chest tipped back his chin and roared. 'Oh, nice one, Granville. I like someone with a sense of humour. Someone who can draw! An artist! No, I mean someone who can draw a Colt 45, like John Wayne or Jimmy Stewart. Hang on a minute; Leonardo, you say. How about Di Caprio? I must give his agent a ring. Remind me, Duchess.'

Teeny put a hand on his arm. 'Be sure I will,' she purred reassuringly. Granville wondered how often she defused Chest by saying she would follow up his wilder ideas and then quietly forget them.

The Manager of *Crowned Crane Lodge* walked up to Chest. 'I'm sorry to disturb you, Mr Trumper, but could I have a word about the arrangements for your safari tomorrow?'

'Excuse me willya?' said Chest irritably and left with the Manager.

He returned a few minutes later looking

disgusted. 'Can't bag a rhino; says they're a protected species. I offered to unprotect them, but Smoothie says it isn't possible under the laws of Zuzubia. If I want to take a pop at a rhino, it's got to be with a camera. Gotta shoot ga-zelles. No honest, I'm telling you, ga-zelles.'

CHAPTER SEVEN

Edwin Chilomba was a jolly man. The youngest member of the Zuzubian cabinet, he was fit, energetic and personable. 'A hartebeest, that's what I am,' he was fond of saying, throwing back his head and laughing with a deep throated chortle.

As Minister of Tourism and Development, he used every excuse to visit *Crowned Crane Lodge*, staying overnight whenever he could. He was an early riser. This morning he'd been up since five, swimming and then spending an hour in the Lodge's gym before breakfast. Being an affable sort, he was always willing to mingle with the guests. But there was an exception to this: the Minister never dined with them. His diet was simple: a bowl of maize porridge in the morning and another at six in the evening. Water, a bit of fruit, a few leaves, and very little else. So while the guests of *Crowned Crane Lodge* were gorging themselves, Edwin Chilomba was pumping iron.

Like all addicts, Odile was a mistress of self-deception. She fooled herself and tried to convince those around her that she was on a diet. Rather than eat less, she shifted the responsibility onto various diet plans. By signing up to them, she salved her conscience. Nothing remained but to ignore them.

The reason why Odile was the only guest still at breakfast this morning was that she could now pig herself alone, whereas in front of her fellow diners she'd had to play out a pretence, picking at her food. It was an indication of how greatly she deceived herself that she genuinely thought, at such moments, that she really was dieting, whereas in reality it fooled no one. Odile weighed nineteen stone.

Odile chose her diet plans with care. They had to be those which gave her some encouragement. 'Be kind to your weight' was comforting, but not as much as 'Go on, spoil yourself.' The companies who pedalled these products knew they were onto a good thing with people like Odile. They knew that what slimmers wanted more than anything was to receive a blessing that they could, indeed should, eat the treats which they'd been told to avoid. So brand slogans such as 'Be kind to your weight' and 'Go on, spoil yourself' were a licence - no, better than that, a command - to those struggling with their consciences to simply give in. 'Go on, spoil yourself, stuff your face. Oh, and by the way, swallow some of these expensive pills with your sixth can of diet cola.'

Kwame, the good-looking waiter, was happy to oblige. The moment he'd seen Odile, his heart had started thumping. He'd been so used to skinny, white-faced skeletons with pointed noses that he'd despaired of ever serving a female guest with a decent amount of flesh. What I would like to see is a lady with a bosom I could hide in and a proper ledge to her bottom. And here suddenly was one who was exactly that, in the shape - and what a shape - of this fine lady. And when she'd stayed behind after the others had left, Kwame realised that, as he was now in Heaven, he would have to behave himself.

He approached her from behind to get a true impression of her girth and be able to inhale within olfactory range of her quivering neck. 'Good morning, Madam, I hope that Madam has reclined satisfactorily in the night?'

Madam seemed to freeze; that is her knife and fork remained motionless while her flesh wobbled to a standstill.

'And how would Madam like to be pleasured today?'

This time the lady twitched. Kwame admired the way a ripple fell from her shoulders to her thighs. Incapable of turning, and with the act of standing up impossible without the rigmarole of heaving herself up by means of the table, she simply sat there, saying nothing.

Kwame peered round the side of her chins. The head turned towards him with a look of such malevolence that he jumped back and fled to the kitchen.

As Kwame hurried through one door, another burst open. The Minister of Tourism and Development swept across the dining room, his gaze alighting on the only person there. He swung right, strode up to Odile and extended a hand. 'I don't think I've had the pleasure.'

'No, and you're not going to get it,' Odile spat at him.

The Minister's smile froze, his eyes popped and his jaw fell. Only his mother and the President had ever spoken to him like that.

'Fetch me some toast, this lot's cold. And I'm still waiting for my fourth and fifth eggs.'

Edwin Chilomba straightened, blew out his cheeks and thrust out his chest. 'You want me to fetch your toast and eggs?'

'Are you deaf? That's what I said.'

'I see.'

'You may see, but I don't detect any movement.'

'Do you know who I am, Madam?'

'I don't care who you are, but I know what you aren't, and that's providing me with service.'

'Madam, I am not...'

Odile heaved herself forward. She turned a quarter sideways and flopped back again, half of her flesh wobbling out over the sides of her chair. 'I want to speak to your manager.'

'My manager?'

'Your boss, you stupid oaf. You know what a boss is, I take it?'

The Minister chortled. 'Oh yes, Madam, I have a boss. He is a very big man.'

'I'm not interested in his size. Fetch him, do you hear?'

Edwin Chilomba looked down his nose and

Odile looked up it. 'Madam, my boss is a hundred miles away.'

'What? Ridiculous.'

'You see, Madam, I am not a member of staff of this hotel.'

'What are you then, a guest?'

'I am sometimes a guest. Today perhaps I am. But then again, perhaps just a visitor passing through. But I am responsible that you should have a pleasant stay here.'

'You're talking in riddles. If you're a guest like me,' Odile looked disgusted at the thought, 'why should you be responsible for my wellbeing?' She was beginning to be curious, if only slightly. At least this man had a more subtle chat up line than that donkey who was in here earlier.

The Minister drew himself up to his full height and puffed out his chest. 'Madam, I am the Minister for Tourism and Development of the Republic of Zuzubia.' He said the name of his country so loudly and so proudly that all the syllables merged triumphantly into one.

'Are you indeed? Well, I'm pleased to meet you.'

'Thank you, and it is an honour to be of service to you, Madam.'

'Yes, well, I hope the service of the country is better than the service of this hotel.'

The Minister turned up the charm. 'I said I was responsible and I meant it. Any failure of service here is a reflection on my country. Now I will deal with your problem. What is your favourite food? Your very best, your most favourite food of all?'

Odile had so many hang ups and secrets in that

line that she found it hard to answer truthfully. She was about to say either salad or cranberry juice when she received a further prompting. 'What you really like best.' He touched the side of his nose conspiratorially. 'Our little secret, just between you and me.'

Odile looked coy. 'Well, I am rather fond of chocolate.'

The Minister beamed. 'An excellent choice.' He'd only once tried chocolate and it had made him sick. 'Now what is your second best?'

'I adore doughnuts, but they are rather...'

'Doughnuts, good, good. With jam in them?'

'I prefer cream.' Odile was simpering like a four-year-old.

'Cream it shall be. And next?'

'I have a weakness for sausages.'

'Ah, sausages. I believe this hotel has a speciality made from the meat of bushbuck. Very tasty. And what sauces do you like best, Madam?'

'Oh a rich toffee fudge, golden brown.' Odile found herself salivating violently.

'I believe you have been waiting a long time for your order, Madam, is that correct?'

Odile managed to put on an impressive act of almost weeping. 'I did ask for toast and eggs a very long time ago,' she whispered.

The Minister paused theatrically. 'Will you allow me one favour, please?'

Odile was in the palm of his hand, a rather ludicrous thought unless taken metaphorically. 'It depends on what it is,' she replied coquettishly.

'Will you give me fifteen minutes?' He held up a

hand in apology. 'Yes, I know you've been waiting far too long, but I think I can make it worth the wait.' He turned and walked through the doors into the kitchen. He returned a minute later. 'I have a car waiting to take me to a very important meeting. I am very sorry, I have to leave you now. Remember, only fifteen minutes?' Before Odile could reply, he'd spun away and disappeared into the reception area.

Fifteen minutes later Kwame appeared with a tray as though approaching a dangerous animal. On the table he put toast, butter and jam. But in front of the lady he placed a dish which had the sort of eye appeal which earned three stars from Michelin. A large doughnut filled with cream and topped with flaked chocolate formed the centre-piece, from which radiated four dark, meaty sausages like spokes of a wheel. Between each nestled a fried egg. Two sauces spiralled round the edges of the plate, one a rich golden colour and the other dark brown. The whole dish was garnished with fresh raspberries and grapes.

Odile gave a massive sigh. She sliced through one of the sausages and pressed it into the centre of the doughnut until it was coated with cream, picking up flakes of chocolate as it went. Then she dipped it into the toffee fudge sauce, thought of doing the same into the yolk of one of the eggs, but decided she couldn't wait. She opened her mouth extremely wide, paused to build up the anticipation, breathing in the aromas. Then she enfolded her lips around the forkful, closed her eyes and entered the gates of Heaven. Kwame, who'd been watching her from just inside the doors to the kitchen, fled once more before she could open them again.

Out in the lobby, Chest Trumper's mood was a considerable improvement on last night. His attire was a mixture of Davy Crockett and Bertie Wooster, so that Granville Summers wondered whether he was going to say 'Yee-ha' or 'What Ho?'

'Couldn't get Leonardo,' he chuckled. 'Agent says he's just signed up to a new movie with two sequels and a prequel. But know what?' His eyes glinted so that it was clear that he was going to be proud of what he was going to say next. Granville was struggling to imagine Jack Nicholson as General Gordon. 'Rutt Revere!'

Granville smiled weakly at him. He'd vaguely heard of Rutt Revere, one of the most eligible leading men in Hollywood, but couldn't have named a single picture he'd starred in. But that said more about Granville Summers than it did about Rutt Revere.

'Rutt's agent thinks he might be interested, and know what, you just won't believe this: he's coming out to join us right here on the banks of this ole river, ain't that something, on Wednesday. He's always said he wanted to shoot a grizzly. Hadn't the heart to tell him they're a protected species.'

A blond-haired god, clearly the safari guide, entered the lobby. Chest picked up a large case. It looked to Granville as though he was about to move hotels, rather than go out on a day's safari, all paid.

Chest saw him staring and patted the case. 'Got fifteen lenses. Full range, from the widest of the wide to the closest of close ups, to see the yellow of their eyes.'

'Our animals are wild,' said the guide quietly.

Chest ignored him. Nothing was going to upset him now that he'd bagged Rutt Revere. 'Come on, let's go put some lead into Bambi's butt.' He fizzed out of the hotel like a disgorging champagne cork.

CHAPTER EIGHT

For some time, the President of the United States had been agonising over the growing influence of the Chinese in Africa. His efforts so far were having little effect. He'd strengthened his ties with the big companies who'd poured millions into his election campaign, and they were paying a fortune from the deepest recesses of their subsidiaries in tax havens for 'consultancy services' to shady individuals who in turn were pumping millions into Swiss bank accounts of African leaders. That was not all. The President had taken measures to promote the kind of laissez-faire capitalism that the US itself had abandoned sixty years ago. Pharmaceutical companies were given tax breaks to pedal medicines which had either been banned long ago in the USA or else were out-of-date. With smoking in decline at home, backing was given to tobacco companies to promote in Africa the healthiness of dragging on a cigarette. Political paths were smoothed so that the conglomerate

Romboserve could market its cola drink containing a vast amount of sugar and three times more caffeine than the legal maximum set by the USA in 1946. The effect on health, and especially children's teeth, was disastrous, which suited Romboserve just fine, as it was also big in dental products. Synergy they called it. Poor Zuzubian peasants were unable to compete against imports from American and European farmers, underpinned by huge subsidies.

But the Chinese still seemed to be gaining ground, sometimes literally as they bought up millions of acres of land in Africa each year. They were the ones winning all the contracts for railways, bridges, and sugar factories, because their managers and workers lived in dormitories and camps, whereas the Americans insisted on staying in expensive hotels with air conditioning.

'What we need,' said the President, 'is to win the hearts and minds of the people of Africa, a Goodwill Ambassador who epitomises the American Way and can be an inspiration wherever he or she goes.' A few suggestions were made to the President, but he rejected them all in favour of Beth-Jo Sorkowski.

Beth-Jo's credentials were impressive. She and her husband, a banker on a seven-figure bonus, were close friends of the most powerful media tycoon in the world. She herself was said by those close to her to be a crack shot and was often photographed posing with one of her ten rifles, although nit-picking critics pointed out that her stance was that of someone who didn't know how to use them. There was never any video footage of her actually firing a shot, only of her standing triumphantly over carcasses, tossing her impressive mane and showing her teeth. She was stridently pro-life and had borne six children by the age of twenty-eight. She had gained the ear of the most powerful TV evangelist in the USA by shouting in it. He was now supporting her campaign to make prayers compulsory before every TV debate, sporting fixture and school assembly in the country. Although the President knew that such legislation was unconstitutional and stood no chance of being passed, he needed to offer her a lucrative post which took her as far away from Washington and the air waves as possible.

The post of Ambassador for the Promotion of American Culture in Africa suited both the President's objectives and Beth-Jo's talents, since she was utterly uncorrupted by any preconceptions about Africa. Beth-Jo had never travelled outside the USA, and would have been hard pressed even to point to where Africa was on a map, let alone any of its countries. South Africa was in the South, presumably, and wasn't Libya somewhere near the Mediterranean, whatever that was, because hadn't we bombed it from somewhere in Europe? Oh yes, and there was Egypt, but perhaps that was in Asia?

With admirable commitment, Beth-Jo had plunged straight into her new role. The day after landing in Zuzubia, she'd mounted a rostrum before a sullen group of women bussed in on the orders of the President. A few of them spoke English, so could understand Beth-Jo's words, if not her sense. 'I'm a working mom, just like you all. I know what it's like to have to drive the kids half a mile to school, get to the hair salon on the dot of nine, and then battle my way through traffic to work.' The ladies had been able to empathise with the task of driving a flock of baby goats, but were surprised to hear that kids in America went to school. They had no idea what a hair salon was and had never driven a car in their lives.

'We moms should stick together!' Beth-Jo threw her hands encouragingly above her head, expecting cheers or at least some polite applause. The ladies looked mildly surprised. Was this some kind of fertility dance?

Interviewed later on Radio Zuzubia, Beth-Jo said, 'I want to raise their standards to what we have in the USA. I want them all to be leaving thirty percent of their food on their plates. I want them to instinctively think 'Doggy Bag' when they go to a restaurant.' When the interviewer politely pointed out that few Zuzubians could afford to get to a restaurant, let alone step inside one, Beth-Jo replied, 'Yea, that's so, so wrong. That really sucks. I want to change all that. We've got to start somewhere and the time is now.' As an afterthought she added, 'I want them to feel comfortable about tipping twenty-five percent and not feeling bad about what's on their credit card.'

Garston Peters read the article with interest. Although he despised her ignorance, her arrogance didn't bother him. He instantly sensed a business and political opportunity. Within an hour, his contact at the US embassy had put him on to Beth-Jo.

'A food eating competition?' she trilled. 'An international food eating competition? Why ain't that coolness itself!'

'How long are you in Zuzubia?'

'Well now, let me see. I'm in Cape Town on the 10th, that's in South Africa by the way, and some place called Abyss Adaba, Abracadabra, oh I don't know.'

'Addis Ababa. It's the capital of Ethiopia.'

'That must be the place, next month. And then I go on to Oochie my Googa, oh these darned names!'

'Where's that?'

'You tell me. Where's anywhere? Some place like Bikini Fatso.'

'There's a country called Burkina Faso, and its capital is Ouagadougou.'

'That must be it then. But hey, look, don't let's worry about that. I could get here on my way back from South Africa.'

They made their arrangements. There was to be an international food eating competition in three months' time. Garston Peters would provide the venue. What he knew, and Beth-Jo did not, was that Edwin Chilomba, the affable and athletic Minister of Tourism and Development, was losing influence with the President of Zuzubia. If anyone should know, it was Garston Peters. He'd done everything he could for Chilomba. God knows he'd tried, offering free membership of the golf club, schooling for his children and vouchers for his wife to spend in some of the most prestigious shops in Paris, London and New York. When all of these had been refused, Peters had offered Chilomba two hundred thousand dollars in cash. Chilomba had turned that down too. Still the bastard had blocked his application for a pipeline to take water from the Tafelka highlands to the new golf course. There was nothing worse than an African with principles. No wonder Zuzubia was so backward, when it could be the African playground of the rich. This stuck-up prig, strutting about on his hind legs flaunting his asceticism, was meant to be Minister for Tourism and Development, for God's sake. He was anti-tourism and anti-development.

A word in the President's ear to the effect that the World Bank would withdraw funding if the pipeline was not built overcame the problem of the pipeline to the extent that the President said he would look into it. And a word in the President's other ear that Chilomba had been spending a lot of time at *Crowned Crane Lodge* without paying seemed to have got round the problem of Chilomba. Edwin Chilomba would never agree to a food eating competition. The man himself hardly ate. But the powerful Minister of Finance, Godson Malembe, who always accepted Peters' gifts graciously, was so enthusiastic he'd probably want to join in. With his eighteen-stone frame, one wouldn't want to bet against him winning. Peters mulled over the idea. An emetic in the other contestants' food, perhaps?

There was another possible boost to the food eating competition. Len McRory, an Irishman based in London, was one of the biggest food magnates in the world. McRory had built up a vast empire in food manufacturing, wholesale and retail. He was a genius at fooling the public. His fatty products were trumpeted as being sugar free, and his sugary products as being fat free. He was master of the meaningless statement. 'Our ducks are allowed to flap their wings and have free access to water.' What was that supposed to mean? That they wouldn't get shot if they dared to flap their wings and wouldn't have to pay for their water? He might as well have written that they wouldn't get beaten if caught quacking. 'Ah yes,' wrote one of McRory's staunchest defenders, paid handsomely of course, 'but only an idiot would think that McRory meant drinking water. What he really meant was water to swim in and wash their feathers.' Only one problem there: McRory's ducks didn't have access to that kind of water. They were kept in cramped conditions but yes, they did have drinking water because ducks, like any other animal, die if they don't drink, which is not good business. His hens, marketed as *Cheapie Chickens* with the slogan 'as happy as the day is long', were reared in horrendous conditions in Brazil to take advantage of an EU trade deal involving quotas. They were fed on locally grown soya, whose acreage increased by the minute as more and more of the Amazon rainforest was felled to make way.

In McRory's stores, kids' cereals were the ones with the most salt and sugar. The words 'eco', 'green' and 'local' were used freely, but were as meaningless and unregulated as 'home-made', 'chef's favourite' and 'from the kitchen'. McRory knew how to manipulate the regulations because he dictated what they were. There was nothing illegal about claiming that his tomatoes were free range, even though the statement was ridiculous, as if his tomatoes were 'free' to walk around, have access to their own water supply and, who knows, allowed to quack. Yes, manipulation of the regulations was easy for McRory. Every time the words 'revisit' and 'the law' were mentioned by a junior Minister, McRory would remind the Chairman of whichever party was in power, or was about to be, that he was one of its biggest donors. A word from the Party Chairman to Number 10, and a word from Number 10 to the junior Minister, and a statement would quickly be issued that no progress could be made without the consensus of the food industry, that legislation was not the answer, and the subject would be quietly dropped for another year or two.

Of course the reason why politicians were so easily bought was that their parties were funded by the likes of McRory and his companies. The obvious answer would be to ban corporate donations to political parties and have them funded by the taxpayer. McRory had that covered too. Every time the subject of political funding was raised, McRory's stooges would bombard the newspapers with letters opposing the idea. Articles would appear, supposedly written by independent journalists, saying things like, 'How dare these incompetent and sleazy politicians demand more money from the taxpayer?' Once more the public was duped into thinking that what was actually in their worst interest was in their best.

Often, greasing the palms of politicians was

unnecessary. The public were so gullible that they settled the issue themselves. That was why he got away with marketing the unhealthiest of cereals to children. 'Oh look, Mummy, *Choco-Poppo-Pops*, with pictures of Boppo the Bear, I love those.' And no amount of information on the label would persuade Mummy, or Daddy for that matter, that a bowlful of *Choco-Poppo-Pops* contained a third of the little mite's daily intake of salt and half her sugar. And it was worthwhile McRory telling his customers that his sliced slimmer's cheese contained less than 1g of carbohydrate for every 30g, because although quite a few of his customers, if they'd thought about it, would know that cheese isn't a carbohydrate product, McRory calculated correctly that his customers wouldn't think about it. The claim simply needed to sound, at the most superficial level, impressive. Conjurors fool their audiences by the use of misleading and diversionary patter. McRory was a master conjuror.

Sometimes McRory's claims fooled a large section of the public simply because they were fools. 'Four times your daily requirement of lecithin in one bar' could only be worth proclaiming if the people buying it were stupid enough to think it a virtue. McRory knew that if he pumped his chickens with water (20%) and sold them for less (10%) many of his customers would go for it, because few of them understood the difference between price and value. Just to make sure they wouldn't think about that, he called them *Value Chickens*.

Garston Peters had found out through one of his spies that McRory would soon be staying for a fortnight at *Crowned Crane Lodge*. Peters, who wasn't an internationally known businessman in McRory's sphere, knew that he would have difficulty setting up a meeting with a man who, after all, would be on a break. But still it was possible. A phone call from Godson Malembe to McRory, saying that there was an opportunity for a trade deal with Zuzubia, and 'I'd like you to meet with a friend of mine, he is a good man, and I believe there may be business opportunities for you' would be too much for McRory to resist.

CHAPTER NINE

The woman who sat in the lounge in the late afternoon was angry, bored, and frustrated. Lola Zabreo had risen to prominence (infamy really, which is often much more lucrative) by proclaiming that all paintings were a reflection of a primitive state, and that mankind should have grown out of them centuries ago. Michelangelo, Rembrandt, Picasso: all liars and perverters of the Truth. She'd further stated that anything which neither moved nor was at least three dimensional wasn't art at all. She'd championed up and coming artists who'd produced such diverse works as a model of the Queen sitting on a potty eating a tube of toothpaste; a catapult which rotated in the centre of a room firing flies into spiders' webs (it was quickly withdrawn following threats from an animal rights group); and a huddle of five nurses gathered round a bed alternately recoiling in shock at the sight of a worm on a patient's stomach. Even detractors admitted there was something hypnotic about the nurses springing back and then peering forward again like those chickens which peck in rotation at a hand-held board.

Another work championed by Lola was a four-hour long recital of sentences without main verbs, such as, 'What one's got to remember, especially in a situation like this, because of the forces, factions and, if I may use this word, using it in an admittedly pejorative sense, which I can only justify by what has gone before, which is really rather difficult.' When a fellow critic had sniffily suggested on a television panel that that was just plain boring, Lola had looked as though she were about to attack him, but instead had put her face into the lens of the camera and hissed through gritted teeth, 'That's the point!' Once she'd supported squalor and boredom at the same time, praising a continuous film of the artist defecating in the left-hand side of a split screen, while a text explaining it all scrolled slowly down on the right.

Lola was rich and a bit famous from her many TV appearances. What she said was usually excruciating garbage, such as, 'Note how the paradigm has juxtaposed itself with its alter ego.' But the way she flung her arms about and alternately shrieked and purred at her audience, together with the fact that she was really rather beautiful to look at, won her many admirers. She dressed well, and had a rare ability to switch in the blink of her lovely brown eyes between being sexy, animated and statuesque. She was influential too, having just secured Arts Council funding for a very surprised young student to build a snowman at the

South Pole. 99.9% of the cost of £42,000 was to be spent on getting the artist there. No one had dared to question her, but many suspected that she would have replied, 'That's the point.'

Lola was a successful author. Each of her books trashed the crackpot theories put forward in the previous one. Reviewers praised her for her flexibility and honesty in changing her opinion, not realising that she did it to make money.

Like many of the guests at *Crowned Crane Lodge*, Lola was fed up with the rain. The brochure and her travel agent had promised clear blue skies, but the rains had arrived a full month early. Although warm, it was dark, gloomy and wet nearly every day. Then, frustratingly, the skies tended to clear at sundown. Today had been the fifth day when she'd been told that it was impossible to visit the Oboobo Tribe.

Teeny Trumper, light as a feather, breezed through the front doors, saw Lola sitting there and floated into the armchair opposite her. The two had got to know each other and, for want of adequate female alternatives, had formed something of a mutual bond.

'You look all of a flutter, Teeny. How's your day been? How's Chest?'

'Oh, he's out there somewhere getting wet, nosing around for animals in the mist. Darning and dratting I should think.' She gave Lola a look which said listen to what I've got to say next. 'As for me, all of a flutter about sums me up. But I got there in the end.'

'You've bought your baby?'

'I have, I really, really have. But it was hard, Lola, they made it as hard as they possibly could. That Mother Superior! We'd already paid sixty thousand for little Benjamin, and still she had the cheek to ask for a donation. I told her we'd got what we'd come for, but still she persisted. "To pay for the others, the ones left behind, perhaps? Nkambadula's friends?" Nkambadula! How dare she say that name when I'd already paid for Benjamin and given him a Christian name! I said I certainly wasn't going to pay any more money unless they brought the place up to scratch. Would you believe they don't even have air conditioning? I need a G & T. Want one?'

Lola nodded. 'After what you've been through, you deserve one.'

'I should say! I felt really stressed in there. I couldn't wait to get away. My Benjamin's so cute, he's perfectly formed, but d'you know some of the others haven't even got arms and legs?'

Lola thought there might be an artistic opportunity there.

Teeny continued, 'Then the Mother Superior brought in a nasty little contracts man who was as bad as she was. We had a right hoedown. I asked him under what circumstances I could change Benjamin, swap him if, you know, things didn't quite work out, and he said I couldn't. Once I'd signed the contract there'd be no sending back. I told him I'd just seen a notice saying, "Baby Changing Facilities", but he wouldn't budge.'

'But in a way that's good,' Lola said soothingly. 'You must feel fulfilled now it's all, well, settled.'

'I do, I do. Anyway, I adore my little Benjamin.

His skin colour exactly complements the drapes in my living room; that's one of the reasons why I chose him.' Teeny's thoughts on that subject were wildly different from Lola's, who regarded harmonious colour schemes as the work of a revisionist devil.

Lola was at least curious. 'When do we get to see him?'

'Oh, he's not coming here. So sorry. They're shipping him over to the States separately.'

'Separately? Aren't you going with him?'

'No, no, we'll take delivery when we get home.'

'But surely someone will be accompanying him?'

'D'you know, I never asked. Hm, good question, but no matter, we've paid so much for him that I'm sure freight'll be included. Don't look so worried, honey. I expect they'll crate him up or something.'

'What about the paperwork? Did that take long?'

'Not a bit of it. Chest got his lawyers to check it out in advance. You see, Lola, the great thing is this: there's just three nations who haven't signed up to the UNICEF Convention on the Rights of the Child: Somalia, Zuzubia and the USA. Sure, there's a lot of paperwork our end. He's got to be stuck through with goodness knows how many needles, I'm so, so glad I won't be around to see it. He'll have to be in quarantine for six weeks.'

Lola wondered whether little Benjamin would be allowed out of his crate during that time. 'And this end?'

'No problem at all. His parents have signed forms to the effect that they're dead and he's really an orphan, but to be honest the Zuzubians aren't that worried. One less mouth to feed.' The gin and tonics arrived. 'So, it's no good worrying about that now. Once we're back home it'll be a real thrill getting to know Benjamin. For now, Chest and I just want to have a good time here and forget all about him.' She took a sip. 'Chest and I have discovered this lovely unspoilt village in New Hampshire with fishing cottages and real fishermen in them. We've bought up all of them.'

'With the fishermen inside?'

Teeny wasn't sure whether Lola was razzing her. She laughed nervously. 'No-o?'

'What happened to the fishermen?'

'I don't know. They've probably moved to Arizona or something. Maybe they're driving cabs now. Anyhow, the important thing is that we got them out.' She smiled indulgently at Lola. 'But look, honey, that's quite enough of me. Tell me what brings you here.'

'My mother died a month ago.'

'Oh my dear, how I sympathise. I know what it feels like. I lost my little doggie Witty the Third last fall. It took me a long time to get over him. But then I told myself, Teeny, you've just got to pick yourself up and get another one.'

Before Lola could wonder how she might acquire another mother, Odile wobbled past pretending not to notice them. Teeny leaned closer towards Lola. 'I don't want to be a gossip but that woman has been seen vamping one of the African waiters. She stays behind at breakfast just so that she can have him to herself if you get my meaning. I should think the poor man feels like diving into the river. Chest calls her the Obeastie. Says if God had wanted hippos to walk on their hind legs he'd have strengthened the boardwalks. Can you believe it?'

Lola couldn't. She looked disgusted.

'Poor thing,' thought Teeny, 'losing her mother and all alone here.' She decided to try again. 'Did I hear you say the other day that you're an artist?'

'More of an enabler, a facilitator of art. I don't like to use the word critic. It sounds so destructive.'

'Oh, don't use the word critic around Chest. He'll be with you on that one. Says they're always looking for the complicated and pooh-poohing the beautifully simple.' Had Teeny known it, that about summed up Lola perfectly. 'What have you been working on recently?'

'We-ll,' said Lola, leaning forward, delighted at the first opportunity in a week to be invited to pour forth, 'my new project is going to be in the London sewers. We're going to plant fifty bowls inscribed with "Save the Whales" at key junctions throughout the network.'

Teeny, who'd sat back at the word 'sewers', doubted whether there really were whales in the London sewers at all. In any case, what would be the point in telling them to save themselves? And if they were already in the sewers, wouldn't it be too late?

Lola smiled indulgently. 'Not the whales; the bowls are there for the rats. Part of the funding is to pay for the daily replenishing of the bowls with food.'

'For the rats? But who will see them? I mean the rats will, but who will be able to read the words

"Save the Whales"?' Teeny was getting seriously concerned about Lola.

'No one will. That's the point, that's the message.'

Teeny thought about Chest quoting Sam Goldwyn the other night, "Messages are for the Western Union" but she was so dumbstruck that all she could say was, 'But the rats can't read. They've never heard of the whales.'

'Exactly!' cried Lola triumphantly. 'That makes it all the more meaningful. We will have made a statement about the interaction between whales, rats and humans and, even more poignantly, the lack of it.'

'I see,' said Teeny slowly.

Lola was so delighted that she thought she'd gained permission to continue. 'But that's not why I'm here, obviously.' She shimmied her shoulders and deepened her voice in a mock Brooklyn accent. 'No rats or whales in Zuzubia. Well, there may be rats...'

'But probably not too many sewers,' Teeny interjected, and the two ladies laughed with delight at each other.

'No, I'm here to look at the artistic potential of the Oboobo people, in particular their fertility dancing and circumcision rituals. But I've also seen photos of the limestone towers which are a phenomenon in this area. They're such fascinating shape potentials. You see, Teeny, we have the ability and inclination to persuade inanimate objects to be our partners in experiences. The boundaries of what I call the mundane are generated by activities acting as oppositional wavelike forces, oscillations that appropriate space through confrontation with values, ideas and encounters...' Lola suddenly noticed that Teeny had a hand clasped over her mouth and her eyes were popping. She turned round slowly to look where Teeny was staring. A youngish man with his back to them was talking to the receptionist. Before Lola could turn back to ask Teeny what the matter was, Teeny had leapt to her feet and was running towards him.

'Rutt,' she screamed, 'Rutt! You're a day early!'

CHAPTER TEN

On a sodden morning which Kirsten would never forget, a bedraggled Obooboan came in half-naked with a small rush pot. He put it down on the veranda and stood back.

Soon after she'd arrived at *Waters of Eostre,* Kirsten had let it be known that she would pay for reptiles and amphibians, ten *dinkwas* for a live specimen, but only one *dinkwa* if it was dead. The large discrepancy was to discourage the locals from killing any animals.

'What is in there?'

Joseph translated. 'He says frog.'

Kirsten leaned forward and removed the lid. Her finger had stopped throbbing from the poisonous thorn of the *mwanajeshi* bush, but the incident had made her wary. It was such a dreary day that she had difficulty seeing inside. Her first reaction was that it was a pile of faeces. She picked up the pot, took it to a small pen she kept for the purpose and tipped out the contents. It still looked like a large poo, slightly darker than flesh-coloured, and featureless. Once it had plopped onto the ground, that was it. She poked it gently with a gloved finger. The side yielded surprisingly far and then regained its shape. Not a turd then. Gently, she rolled it over. She saw immediately that it had short, wrinkled legs with surprisingly delicate feet and what appeared to be a large external bag. But it wasn't moving.

'This animal is dead?'

Joseph translated. The man suddenly became animated. He rushed forward and sort of pinched the poor creature under its neck. The toad (she was pretty sure now that it was a toad) gave a small twitch and then was still. Kirsten asked what it was called.

Joseph translated. 'He says *badooba*.' Joseph glanced at Kirsten and quickly looked down at the ground, half-amused and half-embarrassed.

'Well? What does it mean?'

'I do not think I can say this word.'

'Of course you can. If that's what it's called, that's what it's called.'

'Well, the name it means - I'm sorry, it means - the private parts of a man.'

It didn't look at all phallic. She didn't think that Joseph's English or hers were up to further anatomical description. They called it, what was it, *badooba*? That was all she needed to know for now. She paid the man his ten *dinkwas* and went inside. She booted up her laptop and entered *AmphibiaWeb*, searching on toads. Nothing remotely like it. Next she searched the web for *toads tropical Africa*. Again nothing. She looked in her book *Frogs and Toads of Africa*. No. A little excited now, she pulled down her precious tome, published in 1946 and long out of print, called *An African Odyssey, Explorations of a Wandering Zoologist, Part Three: Reptiles and Amphibians*. Most of the illustrations were exquisite line drawings. There were four plates on frogs and toads, but nothing like the one she'd just seen.

She returned to her specimen. It was quite large, a bit bigger than her clenched fist. Its mouth was wide and its eyes a beautiful golden colour. Most toads had warty skins, but this one was heavily wrinkled, hanging down so that its body was somewhat pear-shaped. She had the impression that if she picked it up, the contents would sink to the bottom, like porridge in a bag. She did so, and that was exactly what happened. She stared at it for a long time. What if...? She went back inside and picked up *Frogs and Toads of Africa* again. Turning to a small section at the back entitled *Extinct Species*, she let out a gasp. *Bufo Sayeri*, discovered by Auguste Sayer (one of her heroes) in 1902, last seen in Uganda in 1951. It listed where and when other specimens had been found. Reason for extinction unknown.

Kirsten walked out onto the veranda in a daze. The rain was coming down harder but she hardly noticed.

'Are you all right?'

'Yes, Joseph.' She had to think carefully. This was sensational, enough to send more than just zoologists rushing to Zuzubia. She must take some photos now and post them on the internet. No, careful. Only those who needed to know must know. Her professor in Kumbala? The others here? Mo would be discreet, Jake anything but. Stanley? Hardly a priority for a toad announcement, although... Kirsten smiled to herself. She wondered. A few privileged scientists in her field, the ones she could trust? There weren't many of them. Only one, in fact, Chuck Larter in Ohio. She returned to Joseph. She needed his help, and she could trust him.

'Joseph, I want you to listen very carefully.'

———

Mo's advice was sound. 'I agree, keep it to just me, Joseph and that one expert you know you can trust. He'll be able to research the toad further without the whole world getting to know before you're ready. I wouldn't tell your man in Kumbala just yet. He'll have to be told sooner or later, but if you're not one hundred percent certain of him, best not for now. I agree about Jake. He won't be able to resist making jokes about it. Tangle will probably fret and fuss, and of course any thoughts of people coming here will upset her qualigens. That will have to happen down the line, but we can prepare her carefully. You ought to think up a code name, something relevant enough to be memorable, but obscure enough not to give a hint as to what you're talking about. The word 'toad' must never pass your lips or mine in public. By the way, what does the thing eat?'

'That's the first problem, I haven't a clue. I'm going to give it a variety of foods: worms, grubs, plants, whatever, but the trouble is that animals which have become extinct are often those with narrow diets. Adaptability is the key to survival, and somehow the toad didn't get it.'

'But it isn't extinct.'

'No, but it's very, very rare. Think giant pandas and bamboo. Joseph's asking the man who brought it to find out more. We'll see.'

Tangle was worrying about Jake. She'd told him to take the van to Kumbala to collect some provisions, but he hadn't returned by nightfall, and it was now ten the next morning. She'd had a frustrating day, no week come to that. The rain was relentless and it was getting her down. There was far too much turbulent energy in the water courses. Also, she'd had an unusual amount of ridiculous correspondence to deal with. First a letter asking for a loan.

'Dear Honourable Lady,

In fact, and in addition to that, I humblefully beg of you to consider my onerous situation. My warehouse, packaging and transport business is far from being workmanlike, due to a bad customer being totally and grossly failing to honour a credit debt owing to my goodself. This has caused hardship of a liquidity nature, due to the aforementioned abominable situation. I am begging you wilfully, Madam, to please lend me only for a short while, so that I can most certainly pay it by return, the sum of six thousand dollars. I shall be for ever in your debt.

Your humbleful and obedient servant, Mr Jollimer Ntusu.'

Well, Mr Jollimer Ntusu, I have no intention of being for ever in your debt. You can humblefully and obediently take it from me that, and in addition to that, I don't have any money either. She wrote back,

'Dear Mr Ntusu,

Thank you for your kind letter, which I read with interest. We are an organisation dedicated solely to permaculture, and our charter does not allow us to partake in any other activities, including banking.

Yours sincerely, Tangwystl Breeze.'

Then there were the emails. Mrs Blanca Patrionas had sent one asking if she could come out to save the donkeys. Tangle had emailed back that there weren't any donkeys at *Waters of Eostre* or, as far as she knew, anywhere nearby. There were plenty of things to be saving, but not donkeys.

Infuriatingly, the wretched woman had still come back to her, not by email, but actually on the phone.

'I specialise in donkeys.'

'Good luck to you then,' Tangle had replied in her Welsh lilt, 'I hope you find them, and I hope they're unwell.'

'Excuse me?'

'You're clearly not looking for fit ones. You can't save them if they're well, can you now?'

Tangle wasn't sure which one cut the other off first.

A few hours later, she had a distressingly similar

exchange with a woman who also wanted to do some saving, this time of people. Tangle was fairly sure the call came from within Zuzubia.

'Are you sure your Africans are fulfilled?'

'They seem perfectly happy to me.'

'But they must be made to realise that their lives are a misery.'

'Are you saying we should take perfectly happy people and make them miserable by telling them how miserable they are?'

There was a long pause.

'Are you sure that they've all found Jesus?'

'Jesus.'

'Exactly.'

'I was swearing. Impose your will on others if you must, but do it for their benefit, not yours. Do not patronise them by telling them you know what's good for them better than they do themselves. The Zuzubian wants his own life, not yours. Goodbye.' Tangle prided herself that, however strong her ethos for *Waters of Eostre,* she never imposed her philosophy on Africans. All she asked was that they should respect her taboos, as she respected theirs.

Then there were the goats. A large number of people in the UK had signed up to a scheme called 'Get your Goat.' Rather than give a Christmas present to friends and family, they would make a donation in their name towards buying goats for villages all over Africa. While their friends and relatives seethed, these worthy people, beacons of the nanny society, basked in the knowledge that they were donating something for the poor Africans to use, rather than money to be wasted on beer and tobacco.

Tangle had forgotten that she'd agreed to act as a contact point for the occasional goat being delivered to her region of Zuzubia. Now, due to a computer error, all the goats for the whole of Zuzubia were being sent to *Waters of Eostre*. The local agent thought it wasn't a problem, as goats are herd animals and would be distressed if the flock were separated. The transport operator thought it was wonderful because his costs had been slashed by delivering them all to one place. The goats thought they were in paradise; billies, nannies and kids altogether, and weren't there so many lovely things to eat?

They'd arrived late yesterday afternoon. Tangle had been meditating down in the Arbour of Peace, Mo had been installing a hand pump below the ravine, Jake had been in Kumbala, or on his way back, and Stanley had just stood there gawping. The driver had simply let down the ramp of his truck, waited till the goats had rushed down, told Stanley to 'sign here' and then driven off. Now they'd gone feral, scattering themselves, qualigens and negative impulses to the four corners. By the time Tangle and Mo had appeared, it was too dark to try and catch them, and they needed Jake, who still hadn't returned.

He eventually arrived back in the middle of the following morning looking dishevelled. 'I feel like a goat: bearded, smelly and at the end of my tether.' It wasn't the right thing to say. Tangle burst into tears, and for one glorious moment Jake thought it was because she was relieved to see him.

'What happened to you?' she wailed. The misunderstanding was spectacular.

'Van broke down twenty miles from here. Couldn't find anyone to call for help. Don't worry.' He put an arm round Tangle. He would have preferred it if Mo and Stanley hadn't been standing there at this intimate moment, but one had to seize one's opportunity. 'There, there, it's all right,' he looked lovingly into her eyes. 'I'm here now, as you can see.'

And smell, thought Mo. What was the boy playing at? Tangle gave a final sniff and disengaged herself lithely from Jake, who allowed a hand to brush across her hip. He beamed at the assembled company. 'Boredom was the worst problem. All I had was the *Times of Zuzubia*. I read a very interesting article on *When to Beat your Wife*. Not whether, mind, but when. It was very learned, very closely argued. A highly convincing case was made. Anyhow, eventually the police found me in the late afternoon. They said my van licence had expired.

'Oh yes, that's right.' Tangle looked contrite. 'Sorry, I forgot to renew it.'

'They took me to a hut and asked for my name and address. I told them: Moshe Guterman, Windy Bottom, Sex Drive, Supercalifragilisticexpialido-cious. You know what they're like, these Zuzubian officials, only capable of writing one letter at a time before you give them the next one. As we completed each word, the sun dropped lower in the sky. We'd just started on Supercali when the sun set. This being the tropics, it got dark quickly, so by the time I'd got to fragilistic he couldn't see to write. He didn't have a lamp or even a torch. So he turned to me and told me I could go. The trouble was I couldn't, so I spent the night in the van. A lorry driver gave me a tow to the garage just as it was getting light, and then brought me on here, all smelly and goaty.'

'Go and have a quick shower.' Tangle had switched to her businesslike mode. 'Ten minutes, no more. There's a flock of goats to round up.'

'Yes really,' Mo told the astonished Jake, 'but they're not as smelly as you.'

CHAPTER ELEVEN

Tangle sat twiddling a pencil in her hair somewhere below her neck. She looked across at Mo through dark eyelashes, her head slightly on one side.

There was nothing unusual about her asking to see him. Mo was used to being approached about all sorts of day-to-day issues; but this time she'd sent a message summoning him to her office, and when he'd entered, she'd asked him to close the door.

'You don't like Garston Peters, do you?' She drew herself up in her chair as though waiting for the blow of Mo's response.

Mo thought fast. The obvious answer was no, he didn't; Peters was scum, and he wouldn't be ashamed to say why. But what he'd learned from Kirsten, who in turn had been told by Joseph, was that Tangle was somehow indebted to Peters. Mo was fairly certain from that visit a fortnight ago, when Peters had talked about Mama Kuli's sauces, that Tangle didn't like him. But she'd shown every sign that she was afraid of him, and Mo could hardly blame her. Rather than answer her question directly, he decided to give reasons which would imply an answer. 'Before I came out to Zuzubia, I did some research on the country: economics, politics and the like. It soon became clear that corruption is endemic at the very top, fuelled by large corporations from outside, aided and prompted by agents and accomplices inside Zuzubia. I kept coming across the name Garston Peters and his company, Enlandia. I didn't think any more about it until I found myself sitting next to him at dinner. When you left the room with Peters, Kirsten told me things that kinda complemented what I'd discovered: villagers forced off their land, moved to places where they have no water, a pipeline being diverted to irrigate his golf course.'

As he'd been talking, Tangle's gaze had wandered from Mo to the gardens outside, barely visible in the gathering gloom. She doesn't like what I'm saying, he thought. The silence which followed seemed to confirm his suspicion.

'I know you think I'm cranky.' The click of her Welsh consonants would have sent Jake into a swoon, and even Mo loved the lilt. She turned her eyes fully onto him. 'Trying to make a living from sustainable horticulture, and trying to make the place peaceful and beautiful, I don't want to spoil it by going into mass production, see?'

'You mean Mama Kuli's sauces?'

'Precisely.' Mo loved the way she said the word precisely so precisely.

'Peters trying to cash in on the organic name without the ethos?'

'Exactly.'

She really is a one-off, Mo smiled to himself. 'I think what you're doing here is simply beautiful. You employ six Africans, and I happen to know that every one of them is proud to be working here.' A flash instantaneous with a shuddering roar shook the house, making them both jump. The lights had gone out. Normally, they would have rushed for the lamps and candles, but Tangle showed no sign of moving.

'Does this mean you're thinking of turning Peters' offer down?' Mo was thinking of what Joseph had told Kirsten, that Peters might make life difficult at *Waters of Eostre* if Tangle didn't go along with him. He decided to gamble. 'Is Peters threatening you?'

Tangle baulked rather less than he'd expected. 'The peculiar thing is, well, yes and no. He hasn't put any demands on me, at least not yet. He hasn't even insisted that I grow the ingredients for Mama Kuli's sauces. I don't want to and I'm not going to. All he said was that I should put my house in order.'

It was so dark between the flashes of lightning that they could hardly see each other. She needed him to be decisive.

At last Mo knew what he needed to do. 'Stall him. Let him know you're thinking about the Mama Kuli scheme. Better still, go along with the early preparations without spending any money and without of course upsetting the beautiful harmony here. Don't sign anything. If you're under pressure, let me know; I may be able to help. Can I ask you a favour? Can you spare me for three days while I go to Kumbala? I want to take Joseph with me. Kirsten's agreed.'

'Yes, yes, take the van. Oh no, it's still being mended, and then there's the licence. No, go with the produce lorry on Tuesday, that will be fine. And... thank you.' Her voice had become cracked. He wondered whether there were any tears which he couldn't see. He felt he was behaving badly as he stood up to go. He knew she needed more comforting, but the atmosphere had become a little too electric. If he didn't break away now, anything might happen. He thanked her and left the room.

Chuck Larter emailed back from Ohio surprisingly swiftly. 'Congratulations, Kirsten. You're really going to throw the spotlight on our world. *Bufo Sayeri* it is, no doubt about it. Lovely pics. Sayer tried to get one home in 1935 or 36, but it died on the ship. Of the six recorded specimens, two were already dead and three died within a few weeks in captivity. The sixth lived for eight months before the voyage. He ate a variety of invertebrates, but still didn't survive long. As you know, most toads are omnivorous in their adult stage. It's a puzzle why this one seems so fussy, but there are many reasons why an animal is rare or becomes extinct other than diet. If you can get some DNA to me, I'll get to work. I suspect it might be related to *Bufo Regularis*, but we can't be absolutely certain that it's a *Bufo* at all yet.

You will of course know that the *Bufonidae* are classed by physical characteristics rather than taxonomy. Put simply, all toads are frogs! It might be a *Xenopus*. I would love to come out and join you. I might still do so, but not for now. It's best if I work on your sample DNA here first. You'll never believe the colloquial name the Africans gave it. *The Scrotum Toad*. Yes, really, and from your description I can see why. The nuptial pads also confirm that it's a male. That makes it really interesting, since toad females are usually considerably larger than males. It would be even more exciting if you found a real whopper!

'Do take care, Kirsten. I need hardly tell you that there are some hellishly poisonous frogs in the world. Love the code name, by the way, Second Coming. Rest assured, I won't use the T word from now on. Your secret's safe with me until you decide to open the floodgates. Believe me, Kirsten, you're going to be famous whether you like it or not.

'One more thing. Have you thought about trying to get hold of some tadpoles? I can't find any record of anyone having seen them. Sayer had a theory, totally unproven, that his *bufo* wasn't a true amphibian. He speculated that mating takes place out of the water. As you know, frogs that do that skip the tadpole stage. Best regards, Chuck.'

Kirsten went to her English-Danish dictionary, wondering what the word *Scrotum* meant. She blushed slightly when she found out.

CHAPTER TWELVE

Granville Summers paid no attention to the two men in the far corner of the lounge. As someone accustomed to staying in exclusive hotels, finding himself in a room with famous people meant nothing special to him. He'd already met Chest Trumper, and as for this fellow Rutt Revere, let the ladies do the swooning over him.

Lola couldn't help her hormones. She'd been timing her entrances to make a stunning and, she'd hoped, favourable impression on Rutt. She entered the dining room in a startling blue gown which had minimal material above her waist and none on her back and arms. She walked slowly and seductively, and as she swung her hips past the table where Chest, Teeny and Rutt were about to place their orders, she nonchalantly but skilfully flung a stole across a shoulder in such a way that an end brushed across Teeny's face. Her profuse apology was graciously accepted by Teeny, who introduced her to Rutt. First mission accomplished.

Odile too was all a-flutter, as she waddled through the entrance to the dining room. Unhoisted, her cleavage flopped on top of her belly. Yes, Rutt did look up at her as she passed; in fact his jaw dropped. Odile smirked out of the side of her chins as she waddled past, also thinking first mission accomplished.

As for Len McRory, the food magnate, he was as indifferent to celebrities as Granville. Rutt didn't present a business opportunity, end of story.

In the lounge next day Chest was finding Rutt hard going. He seemed to be behaving differently from when they'd last spoken. 'So you've finished shooting *By the Skin of their Teeth*.'

'Yep.'

'How did it go?'

'Good.'

'How did you find Melanie Storges?'

'I didn't, she was already there.'

Chest slapped Rutt on the knee. 'You're a real cut-up, Rutt. You know that?'

'Uh-huh.'

'Who was that other broad in that movie? Lucy Waterbutt!'

'Yep, she's fine. But what jerk would give his daughter a name like that?'

Chest gulped. Did Rutt really think that Lucy's father would have chosen her surname? Chest was forced to conclude that Rutt probably did think that.

'So, any more shooting in the pipe?' Chest was praying that the answer would be no.

'Right on, piss in ma pants if I don't get some soon. Line 'em up.' Rutt looked down the barrel of an imaginary rifle.

Chest was mortified. He'd hoped Rutt was free to star in his African movie. In his mind he'd been moulding the character of Gordy to fit Rutt's image. 'What you got in your sights, then?' he asked suspiciously.

Rutt grinned. 'A mean, thumpin' great lion.'

'Lion? Oh, I get it, MGM. Have you signed with them yet?'

'Nope.'

'Look, Rutt, I got this role, a big lead for you.'

'Just squeeze the trigger real gentle, now.' Rutt was still looking down his pretend rifle. 'Kap-ah! When do we start?'

'Well now, I'm forward with my plans,' Chest lied. 'All being well, we could start shooting early next year.'

Rutt opened his fingers to let the invisible rifle fall to the floor. He turned to Chest with a wolfish grin. 'What you talkin' about?'

'This African movie of mine. It's made for you, Rutt.'

'That's what you bin talkin' about? I'm not here to shoot movies, man, not even to talk about them. I'm here to shoot lions: real, stonkin', rip-roaring lions with stripes and big shaggy manes.'

'I get it.' It took a lot for Chest to be embarrassed.

'Not the MGM lion? Real ones!' He regained his composure. He'd learned over the years that movie stars had to be indulged. Go along with them when they're off down their track, then head them gently back later. 'Sure, we can go shooting out in the bush in the next couple of days, tomorrow possibly.' Chest decided to postpone the unpleasant moment when he would have to tell Rutt that he wasn't allowed to shoot lions. Or grizzlies.

'I've done with the movies.'

Chest felt as though he'd been stung in the face. He recovered by repeating to himself that, yes, stars had to be indulged, go along with them when they're off down their track, bring 'em back to reality later, yes.

'My life has changed, Chest, changed for the Good. Thanks to Koota Hoki Sri Badabadanath, I'm done with all them evil ways.'

'You what? Who's he or what's that, for the love of Beelzebub?' It wasn't the right thing to say, and it produced a reproachful look from Rutt, but Chest was exasperated.

'It's the One True Faith, Chest, and it's written by God.'

Chest wondered why God allowed there to be so many One True Faiths and why he wrote so many contradictions.

'On the level, Chest, God created the world last night.'

'He what?'

'I'll repeat it for you real slow, Chest, because it's the Truth, and you're my bud, and I want you to know the Truth. God created the whole world last night.'

'All of it?'

'All of it, in a cloud of saffron.'

'But there's evidence to the contrary. I saw you last night, just after you'd checked in, remember?'

'You didn't, Chest, it's all an illusion. It says in the book of Gemphasis that God created man, and loved him so much that he created the earth and the animals for man to do what he liked with. Oh, and the children of Ham.'

'The blacks?'

'Yer, right, the blacks and the genitiles.'

Chest hadn't seen Rutt so animated since he'd been told he was going to die of bubonic plague before the last great battle in *Sword's Revenge*. 'The genitiles? Who are they?'

'All those who aren't of the One True Faith.'

'And what happens the next night, tonight?'

'What you mean, pal?'

'Right, look, if God created man and the earth last night, what happens tomorrow? Did he create the earth last night, meaning tonight, or two nights ago?'

'You've got me confused, dude.'

He isn't the only one, thought Chest. He'd lost his chain of reasoning, but now found it again. 'Tomorrow night's two nights after you said he created it; therefore the world will be two days old. Either that or he's creating the world every night.'

Rutt didn't know the answer to that, but he did know what Koota Hoki Sri Badabadanath had taught him. 'He created it last night. That's what the Book says, so it must be true.'

'So he recreates it?'

'The Book talks about recreation, that's when you go to Heaven. But you gotta be Good first, and you bet your ass, that's what I'm gonna be.'

'When was this Book written?'

'About five thousand years ago, with a bitty added when his great Prophet spoke two thousand years ago.'

'Long before the world was created. That sure is a lot of nights.'

The sarcasm was lost on Rutt. 'We've built a museum to show how God created the world last night. It cost twenty-two million bucks.'

'Well, ain't that something.' Chest tried to sound impressed, and it didn't really matter that he sounded as sincere as a cuckold saying 'How do you do?' to his wife's lover. Rutt was oblivious.

'Yeah, and the maintenance costs on top of that are half a million bucks a day.'

'You mean a night?'

'No. Say, are you taking the Mickey, Chest?'

'Can't you get God to do it?'

'You are taking the Mickey, you hustler.'

Chest smiled to defuse the tension. He'd never heard Rutt talk like this, but he was darned if he was going to play along with it. 'You say it all costs half a million bucks every day to rearrange the furniture, if you'll pardon the expression. That means last night is always last night.'

Rutt looked at him as if he were simple. 'Ain't

that just somethin'. Last night means last night.' He tutted at Chest's stupidity.

'What I meant,' Chest struggled to control his temper, 'is that if you rearrange the museum every night, that means that the world was created last night and not two, three, four or whatever nights back.'

'Buddy, you sure do catch on fast.'

'Half a million bucks every night, that's a lot of dough. It seems a mite unfair on the poorer nations who can't afford it, ain't that so?'

'This is America.'

Chest ignored the fact that they were in Africa. 'You mean you've created a religion which only Americans can afford to follow?'

'I ain't created nothin',' Rutt said sulkily.

'Your guru or whatever you call him, then.'

'He ain't created nothin' neither. All he's done is revealed the Truth.'

'All right, but back to my point about this being a religion only for the rich.'

'That's what makes us a great nation. Koota Hoki Sri Badabadanath teaches us that God wants us to be rich. He says it's our duty to celebrate the Lord's sacrifice for our sakes by being successful. Prosperity is God's work, poverty the work of Satan, yeah man, Amen.'

Jesus, thought Chest, he's even started to adopt the relentless drone of the true enthusiast. He wondered how, if God wanted everyone to get rich, why he wanted them to get poor again by parting with their money to Mr Hokum so that he could build a huge museum and pay an army of people to shift scenery every night. 'So, Rutt,' he said slowly, dreading the answer, 'does this mean you've quit the movies for good?'

The answer was worse than Chest could have feared. 'Sure thing I have. I'm running for Congress.'

Chest let out a splutter which sounded more like a smothered fart than a raspberry.

'I've got eight sponsors who've committed fifteen million bucks to my campaign.'

'Which party?'

'Republican, for sure. I'm affiliating myself to the Tea Party. My aim is to eliminate poverty. We've got to stop spoon-feeding the poor. I'm gonna be campaigning to slash the education budget so people can teach themselves what's best. Power to the people, not some biggety boss in Washington DC. Social Security and Affordable Care, do away with those so folks can look after themselves. That gives them, what's that word they told me? Aspirations! I'm gonna do away with the police, so it's the people who will combat crime. That's why crime's so high, because not enough ordinary citizens have guns. They're doin' nothin' about it themselves, just leavin' it to others. It's the leave-it-to-the-other-guy culture, and I'm gonna put the train into reverse before it hits the buffers.'

Teeny came up to them. 'Have you boys finished your man talk? I bet you're all excited about getting to ride camels and elephants. Don't let the old hog bully you, Rutt.'

Chest Trumper felt like weeping.

CHAPTER THIRTEEN

Kwame approached the Lady with a beaming smile. 'Is Madam feeling fresh today?' Madam ignored him. Her porky eyes were glinting, staring dreamily across the room to where Rutt and his entourage were having breakfast in the far corner. 'I trust Madam had a good lay last night?'

Odile had taken to breakfasting earlier so that she might sit swoonily gazing on the object of her desire. Rutt was half-facing her, but was careful not to look beyond the confines of his table. Fame had taught him that wandering eyes could easily be caught and misconstrued. Even so, a couple of mornings earlier, Odile's had managed to lock into his briefly. Her flesh had tingled when he'd not looked away instantly. It was a lot of flesh to tingle. He'd clearly been fascinated by her. So when he'd turned in his chair to face away from her and look directly at Chest Trumper, she'd correctly identified herself as the cause of this movement. Playing hard to get, good sign. Rutt must have been transfixed by her.

Kwame was still standing there. 'The usual for Madam?' Odile's chins nodded in turn. When he returned with a plate piled high, as artistically displayed as when Minister Chilomba had first ordained it, Kwame could see that something was wrong. Her deflation was almost audible. 'Is Madam nauseating?'

Odile put her podgy arms on the table and gazed at him bleakly.

Kwame felt so inclined to reach out to her emotionally that he ventured, 'Madam, I feel for you.' Rashly, he also succumbed to the impulse to reach out to her physically. He put a hand on hers.

Odile stiffened, well, not exactly stiffened, that was something she could not achieve, but she froze. 'You'd feel for anyone. Get your hand off me.' She peered round the table. 'Where's my toast?'

Appalled, Kwame realised that he'd overlooked it. 'So sorry, Madam, so sorry, I will get it immediately from backside.' He bustled off to the kitchen.

Returning with the toast, Kwame saw ahead of him a tragic sight. Madam was weeping. Cursing himself that he'd been so careless in forgetting the toast, he nevertheless felt a strange thrill that he'd been the cause of a reaction which showed Madam to be so feminine and vulnerable. He felt unbelievably protective towards her, so drawn to her that his desire to touch her again became overwhelming. 'Would Madam like lifting from the breakfast table?' His joy, his disbelief that this was really happening, flooded through him because she'd actually, yes she really had, nodded her consent. Losing all control, he added, 'Would Madam like to come with me, to a secret place, to where...'

Odile wasn't listening. Like some tragic Shakespearian duo, Lear perhaps and his Fool, they shuffled up the aisle of the now deserted dining room in a contradiction of excitement and despair, Kwame imagining the incredible and Odile dwelling on the cause of her grief. As he'd walked past her table, Rutt had sneered at her with a look of contempt and disgust. It was an expression he'd perfected on the set of *Portals of Hell.*

Through the doors, Kwame attempted to steer Madam to the right. She stopped, peered at him and slapped his face, hard.

In a private meeting room near where Odile and Kwame had parted to go their miserable ways two hours earlier, a very different exercise in humiliation was taking place.

No one who ever did business with Len McRory had ever seen him smile, and he wasn't smiling now. With his short thick neck, bull shoulders, letterbox mouth and fender of a chin, McRory exuded power. Garston Peters' tactics, now shot to pieces, had been to lure McRory into a sponsorship agreement involving the food eating competition. This, he'd hoped, would pave the way for future import-export deals. He'd started by trying to impress McRory with tales of his influence within Zuzubia, presenting himself as Mr Fixit, to whose tune the Zuzubian President and Cabinet danced and jumped. Next, he'd tried to woo McRory with his entrepreneurial credentials, with a bias towards food of course, and had told him about his plans for Mama Kuli's sauces. Peters had been prepared for an uphill struggle to gain McRory's interest. What actually happened, with a speed which knocked his breath away, was that McRory charged him like a rhinoceros poked out of its slumbers by an injudicious stick. Before he'd known where he was, McRory was firing contractual terms at him which completely and irrevocably bound Mama Kuli's sauces into the food eating competition and much else besides. Onerous terms were heaped upon onerous terms, but Peters was astute enough to know that the biggest disaster facing him involved deadlines. The food eating competition was barely two weeks away. McRory's game was blazingly obvious, but none the less scary for that: agree to my terms or the whole deal's off, and you haven't got time to negotiate.

Peters tried to wrest back some control. 'I've got an excellent solicitor in Kumbala. I'll get him to draw up the contract.'

'I'll write the contract. You'll have the draft by Wednesday night. That gives you three days to agree it and sign, and a week to implement it.'

'That's very little time to iron out...'

'You're the one who's come to me at short notice. If you don't want to proceed, say so now. I came here to relax.'

Peters couldn't imagine McRory relaxing. 'Can I run through the terms one more time?'

Instead of agreeing, McRory launched into a summary himself, hammering like a machine gun jammed in the firing position.

'Food eating competition. All food outlets within a ten-mile radius of the stadium to be closed for the day. That includes shops, bars, and restaurants. No advertising to appear on anyone's clothing inside the arena except mine. No food or drink to be brought into the stadium. Only my products to be sold. You provide the vending stands and forty staff, I'll provide the products. You erect two thousand of my posters around the town and surrounding countryside by the 14th. My man will fly out with them the day after tomorrow. You also provide two electronic screens at least five metres square, for exclusive advertising of my products. My man will tell you what to do. You're responsible for bussing the punters in from the townships. There'll be a scaled penalty clause if you don't hit twenty thousand. You're responsible for air fares, first class accommodation and all other expenses of the international competitors. You provide the live music, but my man will have a say in that. Now for the food. I'll provide four kilos per competitor, maximum eighty competitors. I have total control over food left over. That Sorkowski woman wants to make an opening speech? Make sure she doesn't get carried away. Pull the plug on her if she gets windy. You say they insist on that Aussie MC, what's his name, Shane Dunster? Done it before? Got a following, not just around the world, but popular here? Hm. Got a house in Kumbala? Good, he should pull them in, then.

'Mama Kuli's sauces. Contract to provide a hundred thousand bottles within eighteen months at fifty-five cents a bottle, wholesale, delivered. Mix of flavours to be specified by me within six months of delivery. I retain exclusive marketing rights for the whole of the USA, Canada, and Europe with options on the rest of the world excluding Zuzubia. You guarantee the products meet the law in all respects in those regions and fully satisfy their organic credentials.

'Future business. You give me first refusal on all food import-exports to and from Zuzubia on any contracts from now on. Happy with that?'

Garston Peters couldn't think of a word which described his state of mind more inappropriately than 'happy'. He was terrified. He told himself he ought to be elated. He'd just struck an exclusive deal, several rolled into one, with one of the most powerful businessmen in the world.

But it felt as though Peters' stomach had risen to sit heavily against his throat. McRory had locked him into not only the food eating competition, but also the marketing of his dream, Mama Kuli's sauces, and had a huge foot in the door of the whole of Zuzubia's future food imports and exports. The trouble was that the foot belonged to Len McRory, and Peters could feel his own toes being crushed somewhere beneath. The timescales appalled him. He'd already known he'd be pushed to get everything done in time for the food eating competition, now only a fortnight away. But that was before McRory had heaped his extra terms onto him. And now the demands which he himself had placed on Tangwystl Breeze, which he'd dreamed up just to put the wind up her, had been crystallised by this maniac of an Irishman.

The time for leaning on Tangwystl had passed. He must jump on her.

Shane Dunster had shot to fame in Australia ten years ago. Following his TV nature programme, sales of tissues had soared, replenishing stocks which had been dabbed into the corners of millions of eyes. Whole households had sobbed as Shane had described what can happen when cuteness and brutality in nature collide. Many had howled in their grief.

'There's only one word to describe this place where I am tonight: paradise. Moonlight is flooding the beach. The only sound is coming from the waves gently caressing the sand along the shoreline behind me. Otherwise all is still. Yet something is stirring tonight, something mysterious and timeless, the awakening of new life. Can you guess what it is, here beneath the sand? Oh heck, I'm starting to get emotional. Can you guess? You've got it, baby turtles, and tonight's the night when they begin their great adventure. We've taken up a good pozzy so we can see them as they emerge. And you're going to see them too. Come in closer, that's right, let's take a squiz.

'Abandoned by their mothers, they've survived

for two months in the sand, potential prey to some of the vilest predators on earth: monitor lizards, dingoes and yes, I'm ashamed to say, us humans. Now, under a full moon, the survivors are emerging, look, see this little critter now, clawing his way up out of the sand. He's made it to the surface; now he must find the sea. There it is, down there, he can sense it, he can hear it, and he can feel the slope of the beach. Come on, faster. Look at his little legs go, that's it, he's really pressed the panic button now. No, fate's not with him, he's a gonna to that crab. Crunch. Ouch. It's heart-breaking. How about this one? She's halfway to the surf already. Go, baby, go. Can she make it? Nope, a bird, was that a gull? Can't be, it's night time, maybe an owl of some kind, didn't even land, just swooped her up in its talons. Farewell my little darling. Sleep in peace. Is there a turtle heaven? I hope so. Now this one, he's already made it to the water, whoops, mind that wave. Need to improve on your surfing skills, mate. Swim, my little gorgeous, swim. What the (beep) was that? Did you see it? Was it a fish or a croc? It moved so fast! Well, he's gone now. This is heartrending.

'Look, the nest's empty. Did any of them make it? Did you see any of them actually get there without being swallowed up? I didn't. What? We've missed one? There he is, halfway down the beach. Good onya little fella, you're within a cooee of the waves. Give him a fair go you nasty predators. Come on, that's right, you little ripper. Hey, whatya doing? Why stop? Oh God, that monitor lizard, it's huge. Oh no, I can't bear it, our little hero's come a gutser.' Shane's voice was choked with emotion. 'Viewers, please try to realise. This is nature. Yes, I know the turtle's a cutie and the great lizard is, well, a monster. But he too's gotta eat. Try and empathise with him, see it from his point of view. To him the baby turtle's just food. Can you relate to that?' Shane Dunster started bawling into the lens, transmitting his grief to half of Australia. 'Neither can I!'

He took his time recovering. 'Now what have we here? A new nest and this time they're coming out together. Good tactic. Safety in numbers. Look, they're on the charge. Look at them go. Now this is what we want. I'm a TV chef, and these little fellas are on my menu tonight.' The camera panned onto Shane, who was tossing what looked like baby turtles in garlic butter.

The letters, phone calls, emails and tweets of protest had poured in, exceeding even the sale of Kleenex in volume. Fury is a public duped while in a state of collective emotion. But the ratings soared. Capitalising on his success, Shane made a smart move. He became a real TV chef. He couldn't cook, but boy could he bully. The way he humiliated those who worked for him made him a superstar. He reduced most of them to tears every night. He didn't have a catch phrase, but his minions did: 'Yes, Chef,' blubbered through quivering lips. His swearing was legendary, so that by far his commonest ingredient was 'beep'. Millions tuned in for the pleasure of seeing a *commis chef's* or a *chef de partie's* bollocks being terrified out of the frying pan into the fire.

Shane then turned his talents to quiz shows. Here he did have a catch phrase. As contestants were eliminated, he would roar at them, 'You're a fucking loser, get out!' (Beeped where appropriate, of course). He hit a rich seam by exploiting Australians' fears about immigration. Three young immigrants were invited onto his show. Each was asked three questions. The first two were simple, even for someone who only spoke broken English. As each was successfully answered, a curtain was lifted a bit at a time to reveal the contestant's mother, flown in from across the world, first up to her waist and then up to her shoulders. Both mothers and contestants were encouraged to call out to each other. There were tears and, 'I love you, Mamma', 'My Darling Baby' and, 'Is it really you?' But the last question was a pig. 'How many vertical struts are there on the Sydney Harbour Bridge?' Or 'What date to the nearest month did myxomatosis come to Australia?' Of course none of the contestants had a clue. The mothers were sent home to the Philippines, Belarus and Moldova without the contestants even glimpsing their faces. The country was divided. Half sobbed their hearts out, and half muttered, 'Good thing too.'

After that success, it was inevitable that an even bigger TV audience should tune into Shane's next show. Five infertile couples desperate to adopt were made to compete for one unbelievably cute baby. The pre-show advertising stressed the all-or-nothing nature of the contest: 'One couple will take home the baby of their dreams, the others will walk away with nothing.' Each couple had to lay it on with a trowel how wonderful they were. Affluence was a criterion; not, as it turned out, so that they could afford to spend sums on the baby, but so that they could display their status and bling. 'My BMW has an electrically operated sun roof,' proclaimed one father, ignoring the fact that the baby would hardly put that near the top of its list of priorities. Voting was done by a combination of audience participation and the number of howls from the birth mother, who was present throughout. Her pleas that she should be allowed to keep the child added piquancy to the show, although her $2m contract prohibited it.

That had been five years ago. Shortly after, Shane had bought a mansion on the outskirts of Kumbala. He'd fallen in love with Zuzubia and had poured huge sums into helping its people build hospitals, clinics, and schools. He was worshipped by the local population and feared by the ruling elite. As Zuzubia's greatest benefactor, Shane could get away with pointing out things to the President which no member of the cabinet dared raise. These days he spent his time between Kumbala, his flat in Sydney and putting in highly lucrative appearances as Master of Ceremonies at major events around the world. His latest had been to compère a food eating competition in Dubai. So with that experience, his gift of the gab, and his presence and popularity in Zuzubia, Shane was the obvious candidate to front the food eating competition in Kumbala. One cannot blame Beth-Jo for approving the recommendation put to her. It's just that, had she or her staff done a bit more research, they might have uncovered the fact that Shane, although he loved Zuzubia and its people, and despised the corruption of those who exploited them, was a loose and potentially destructive cannon.

To Tangle, pulling at her hair with a flicking finger and frowning angrily, Mo was being unsympathetic and cocky. The moment he'd returned from Kumbala in the produce van, she'd called a staff meeting. Kirsten and Joseph had been allowed to attend. Although fighting tears, she'd bravely stood before them and told them her terrible news. Her dream at *Waters of Eostre* was about to end and she would have to dismiss them all.

'I've been told by Garston Peters that I have a choice. I must sell *Waters of Eostre* to him or he will see to it that we cannot sell our produce.'

Jake reacted quickly and angrily. 'That man, what's he doing to you? What's he said? He can't!' He turned to Mo.

'What he has said,' Tangle replied slowly, 'is that the Zuzubian Government has insisted that Mama Kuli's sauces will be manufactured here on commercial lines,' she spat out the words which needed her Welsh accent to convey her full disgust, 'and it has to be up and running within twelve months. I'm not going to do it!'

'Good for you.' Jake was getting really animated now. 'And if you don't?'

'As I've said, the Government will close me down.'

'Bastards!'

'That's crap,' said Mo quietly.

'That's not all.' Tangle seemed exhausted and ashamed. To Jake she looked violated. He longed to protect her. 'He's offered to buy it.'

'The thieving sod!' Jake was rushing towards her.

'For a million dollars.' She neatly side-stepped him.

Mo was unfazed. 'Well, well, how about that?' Even Stanley was a bit shocked that Mo wasn't more sympathetic. 'And how much would you say *Waters of Eostre* is worth on the open market?'

'Oh, I don't know.' Tangle seemed irritated by Mo's question. 'I haven't thought about it. Half a million? No, that's too much. Oh, I can't think about it.'

'I can,' said Mo quietly. 'It's all a load of bullshit. It won't happen, and here's why. Joseph and I haven't been doing nothing in Kumbala. Do any of you know about an international food eating competition taking place there next week? No? Well there is. Peters has sold the idea to a weird woman called Beth-Jo Sorkowski, who's a *balabusta* of a roving ambassador for my country, I'm ashamed to say. The US is kinda sponsoring the whole thing; I almost said controlling it, but in my opinion the whole thing's out of control already before it starts, and it's going to rebound on Garston Peters.'

Tangle and Jake gasped in unison.

'I've met a man called Shane Dunster. He's an Aussie who lives a lot of his time in Kumbala. This Sorkowski woman has appointed him to lead the food eating competition, a sort of Master of Ceremonies if you will. Dunster can't stand Peters, hates his guts. He loves Zuzubia and lays all the corruption here at the door of Peters. He's determined to use the food eating competition to denounce him publicly, and wants me to help.' Mo paused for effect. 'You bet I will.'

'Can we help?' Jake had leapt from Tangle's side to Mo's.

'You most definitely can. All of you can. But that's not all. I said the US Government was sponsoring the event. That's only partly true. Peters has just signed a contract with Len McRory, one of the biggest food magnates in the world. Anyone heard of him?'

They hadn't, but Tangle said she'd met Shane Dunster once.

'You'll know McRory's products, *Chips on Fire, Cheapie Chickens,* but that's by the by. The important news is that McRory and Peters have signed a contract to sew up all the exporting and importing of Zuzubia's foodstuffs, the food eating competition and... Mama Kuli's sauces.'

This time even Stanley gasped.

'Peters is desperate because McRory's imposed terms on him which mean he's got to deliver on everything or get nothing. And he's got to deliver on time. We've got opportunities to trip him up, and delaying tactics will be deadly. First we've got to concentrate on the food eating competition. Here's what I've agreed with Shane.'

When he'd finished, his deeply impressed audience was awed into silence.

Eventually Jake asked, 'How do you know all this? Sure, you got most of it from Shane Dunster.

But how do you know about the contract between Peters and what's his name?'

'McRory. I'm afraid that's the one thing I can't disclose. Shane's sworn Joseph and me to secrecy. Sorry.'

What Shane had told Mo was that there was a mole high up in Peters' company, Enlandia, who was feeding information to Shane. That was how he knew the details of the contract between Peters and McRory even as it was being drafted. Even Mo didn't know the identity of the mole. And Mo mustn't even disclose his or her existence.

Stanley raised a hand tentatively. 'Can I do something, please? I'd like to help, if I can.'

'You most certainly can, Stanley. I already have something in mind, something very important for you to do.'

CHAPTER FOURTEEN

Mo Guterman, Godson Malembe, Garston Peters, Shane Dunster, and Len McRory might have been a mixed bunch, but they all shared a sense of relief that the Great Day had dawned dry and sunny without a cloud in the sky. The forecast confirmed it would stay that way until late afternoon, when there was a risk of heavy thunderstorms.

If Garston Peters was pleased with the weather, he was ecstatic to see a stream of packed buses pouring into the parking areas around the stadium. It was clear that he was going to exceed his target of twenty-thousand spectators. What he didn't know was that some of the buses had been commissioned by Shane Dunster and filled with specially selected Zuzubians of his own choosing.

The stadium looked like a large cow pat which had plopped onto an area of open scrubland three miles from the city centre. It had no architectural merit; in fact it had no features at all other than its stands. The scarlet flowers of three flamboyant trees provided the only colour outside. Inside, Peters had done a reasonable job of creating a sense of style. A VIP area bracketed by glass panels was surrounded by flowering plants in the colours of the Zuzubian flag. Alongside, a large press gallery was already starting to fill. A military-looking man with a large moustache and fierce eyes was addressing a line of stewards in maroon uniforms. They stood respectfully clasping their hands in front of them like footballers protecting their goolies at a free kick. A long row of tables and chairs was set out for the contestants. At either end of the stadium, two large screens, well in excess of McRory's stipulated dimensions, awaited the action.

The stadium was a turmoil of preparation, with a film crew setting up their equipment, porters loading cases of food into the store next to the kitchen, stall holders erecting their stands, electrical engineers carrying out tests on the PA system, and beautiful ladies in long African dresses beginning to set the tables. If Peters had peered past the microphones in front of the rostrum to the right of the VIP stand, he would have been surprised, concerned even, to see Mo Guterman there. He would have had to peer very hard, because Mo was heavily disguised, wearing a blond wig and false moustache. But in any case, Peters' eyes were on a roving tour of approval, taking in the big picture with satisfaction.

The Kumbala Police Band, having finished the National Anthem more or less at the same time but in tonal disharmony, was marching off. Before everyone had finished sitting down, Shane was launching into his speech of welcome from the rostrum. Fluent in Swahili, and speaking more than a little Obooboan, he alternated between three languages effortlessly, without seeming to prolong or bore.

'We're honoured to have with us today Mr Godson Malembe, Minister of Finance. Mr Malembe has a surprise for you all, a real treat, no I'm not saying what it is yet, but I will tell you this: he's a real sport. We're also delighted to have Mr Edwin Chilomba, Minister of Tourism and Development. Mr Chilomba has graciously agreed to say a few words to you during one of the intervals later on.

'I'd also like to welcome Mrs Beth-Jo Sorkowski, who is Goodwill Ambassador of the United States of America. Mrs Sorkowski, who insists I call her Beth-Jo, isn't that right Beth-Jo, will open the proceedings shortly. But before I hand over to her, I'd like to pay tribute to the man who's responsible for everything that's happening today. It's his baby, and without him there wouldn't have been a food eating competition. It was his idea, and he judged that it was just what Zuzubia needs. I give you Mr Garston Peters!' Peters stood up hesitantly in the VIP box and gave a self-conscious bow. 'So, if it all goes wrong, we'll know who to blame, eh Mr Peters?' There was a long pause. 'Just kidding, mate. Right, that's quite enough ear-bashing from me. I'm going to pass you across to Beth-Jo to say a few words.'

Beth-Jo smiled coquettishly at Shane as she replaced him on the rostrum. 'People of Zuzubia! You look swell. What honest round eyes you've got.' (Her brief from Washington had been to denigrate the Chinese whenever she could, but to do it by implication rather than direct criticism.) 'I'm so grateful to you people for tearing yourselves away from your apartments and swimming pools. Isn't this a great day? All I want to say is that this is meant to be fun. Fun for the contestants and fun for you guys. But if I can be serious for just one moment, today is about food, and food can be a serious business. Starvation is an ugly word. I know it's not always easy for you guys to get enough. But we want to help. Today's event is about showing you the way. These people you see in front of you, they're champion eaters, and most of them have flown in from all over the world, especially from my country, the USA. I want to say in all modesty that we lead the world in this. These guys are ready to start eating big-time. They're going to show you how. I want you to watch them carefully and learn from them. Right, it's time to get started. I'm going to hand you back to Shane now to get the contest under way. Shane.'

Beth-Jo looked round in horror to find that Shane wasn't next to her. 'Shane?'

He burst from the stands over on the far side, running out onto the pitch with a hand-held radio microphone. 'G'day Zuzubians, you lovely people. Right, you can see our row of contestants, sixty-two of them they tell me, I never could count beyond ten. And look who we have here in the sky-blue suit, it's our very own Finance Minister, Mr Godson Malembe. Are you really taking part, Sir?'

Malembe hauled his vast frame upright and bowed several times to the ends and sides of the stadium. 'Good onya, Sir, you're a real sport. Now, let me tell you what the contestants are going to be doing. In this first round they have thirty *Chippy Choco* bars, there they are on the big screens, and six equal size bananas. These guys have got to get that lot down within fifteen minutes. They can drink as much water as they want while they're doing it. Any of those that don't finish in time will be eliminated. The rest go through to the next round. Simple, eh? But before we start, a word about a rather delicate matter. How can I explain this? Put simply, the contestants are allowed repeaters, but anyone who throws a pavement pizza's out, eliminated, no questions asked. Now for those of you who don't speak Australian, which I guess is the majority, that means they can belch, pardon ladies, and the other thing, but vomiting, sorry, I couldn't avoid spelling it out, leads to their marching orders, out, finis. Right, that's discharged that one as they say and that's quite enough yabber from me. Are all the contestants ready?' A steward looked up and down the tables. Malembe had lowered his head over his food as though he were going to plunge in mouth first. The steward raised her arm towards Shane, who bellowed, 'Go! Bog in!'

Chippy Choco bars, bananas and water were bundled into mouths. Cheeks bulged like greedy chipmunks. Shane kept up a prattle of small talk at which he excelled, unintentionally diverting his audience from a group of people who had surrounded Godson Malembe, shielding him from public view while one of them, like the conjuror he was, spirited away four of the bananas and fifteen of the *Chippy Choco* bars. So far, Peters' orders were being carried out successfully.

'Stop eating! Time's up.'

Malembe sat back with a smirk. Eleven of the sixty-two contestants had been eliminated in the first round, but not the Minister of Finance.

'Bad luck to those who didn't make it and congrats to those who got through, especially you-ou, Mr Malembe. Isn't our lovable Minister a star? Now, I want to use the time while our adorable young ladies prepare for the next round to tell you something of our sponsor today, Mr Garston Peters and his company Enlandia. We owe him so much. He's built some of the best hotels and country clubs in Africa from scratch. He brings wealthy people from all around the world to Zuzubia. Mr Peters treats them well, extremely well. He protects them. He puts up notices warning that it's dangerous to go beyond the fences of his hotel. D'you know what he tells them?' Shane was alternating between English, Swahili and Obooboan. 'He tells them that if they go out in the bush, they may get attacked by Zuzubians. He tells them that you, the people of Zuzubia, are violent robbers and thieves. Is that what you are?'

A few people shouted back, 'No!' in various languages.

'But don't be too critical of Mr Peters. These tourists bring their wealth, and they spend it here in

Zuzubia. Where do they spend it? In the hotels, of course, because they're told that they must never stray beyond the guarded and fenced area of the hotel grounds. So who gets the benefit of these wealthy tourists' money? Do you get any, you the people of Zuzubia? You don't get one *dinkwa*. It's all spent with Mr Peters and his Enlandia company. Remember, Mr Peters built his holiday complexes from scratch. That took some vision and some bold decisions. In one place he had to force a hundred and thirty people off their land to a place forty miles away, where they have no water at all. That took some courage. See those piccies?' The two huge screens showed a column of Africans shuffling in a dejected line, flanked by police. 'These poor people can no longer visit the graves of their ancestors. And they have no water.' A lone cameraman had walked out onto the pitch and was taking close ups of Shane. 'Now I'd like to introduce you to Mrs Tsala Ndano. She's one of the people forced off her land, together with her daughter and baby son.' Shane slowed his voice. 'The baby died from malnutrition and dehydration. He had no water. Is that right, Mrs Ndano? Take your time.'

Mrs Ndano's face appeared in close up on the big screens, nodding miserably. There was shuffling in the stands behind her, where her extended family, bussed in by Shane, were starting to stir. Mrs Ndano's face faded from the screens. In its place was a meltingly adorable picture of a baby boy. It wasn't hers, because her own baby had never been photographed, but that didn't matter. The effect on the crowd was cataclysmic. Women all round the ground started ululating above an angry buzz of male voices.

Unable to believe at first what he was hearing, and mesmerised by what he was seeing, Garston Peters was slow to react. The only power of authority he could trust to put an end to this attack was Godson Malembe. But he was thirty metres away and very much not to be disturbed. Without knowing what he was going to say, Peters started clambering over the legs of his fellow VIPs, aiming for the rostrum and the microphone where Beth-Jo had made her opening speech. When he got there, he found that the mic was dead. He fiddled with the on-off button and then started scrabbling amongst the controls below. But Mo had done his work well. He'd not only unplugged the cable to the fixed mic, but he'd removed it totally. The only person with the power to address the crowd was Shane, and he was a hundred metres away.

It was time for the second round of the competition. Someone else was doing their work well. Kirsten, wearing an ankle-length dress of bronze and red with matching bandana, was serving the table occupied by Godson Malembe and three other contestants. Her administration of the drug *flunitrazepam* into Malembe's water was both gradual and discreet. Malembe had no idea why he was smiling to himself, for the simple reason that he was unaware that he was doing so. He only knew that he'd started to feel dreamy and that the stadium had sort of expanded and withdrawn to a far horizon.

The second round of the contest was now under

way. This time elimination wasn't on the basis of failing to eat a certain quantity in a given time; rather it was a straight race. The first twenty contestants to despatch their food would qualify. The course was solely fishcakes, nine of them, and they weren't small. There they were on the big screens. *Fishy Funcakes*. Len McRory, who'd risen out of his seat at the sight of the photo of the baby boy, subsided when he saw one of his products.

'This mob look as though they mean business. Those fishcakes are flying off the plates. It's hard to tell who's ahead at this stage. Speed the wombats, there's one who won't be making it to the next round. One of the contestants has yodelled all over the table. Too right, mate, leave the party. Ugh, someone's going to have to clean that chunder up. Glad it's not me. The poor bloke on his right looks rooted. It's all right, cobber, you don't have to finish the extra bit that's landed on your plate.'

The race over, the names of the twenty contestants who'd qualified for the next round were read out. Amongst them, miraculously, was Godson Malembe, now looking more woozy than ever. He'd only eaten three fishcakes, the other six having been spirited away by Peters' conjuror. Kirsten, seeing the state the Minister was in, reduced the dosage of *flunitrazepam*.

Shane strode towards the VIP stand. 'And now I want to invite Mr Edwin Chilomba, Minister of Tourism and Development, to join me out here to say a few words. Please step down, Mr Chilomba.'

As the Minister bounded down the steps, Shane started walking rapidly backwards, so that by the time Chilomba caught up with him they were somewhere near the middle of the pitch. 'Now, Mr Chilomba, Sir, we've known each other a long time. I think I can safely say that we both love Zuzubia?' Shane repeated it in Swahili and Obooboan while Chilomba beamed and nodded. The crowd cheered.

'Would you agree with me that the government of Zuzubia works hard to serve its people?'

Chilomba replied in three languages, 'Yes, definitely.'

'And am I right in saying that you have had to fight against corruption from bad people who are not Zuzubian, and who do not have the interests of Zuzubia at heart?'

'You are right.'

Over at his table, Godson Malembe smiled benignly and sleepily. There seemed to be a deep voice speaking from afar. He wondered if it was God.

'Now, we have heard earlier how poor villagers have been deprived of their basic right to water, because of priority being given to golf courses and other playthings for rich foreigners. Is it true that you turned down an application from Mr Peters' company Enlandia for a pipeline to take water from the highlands to supply yet another golf course planned by Mr Peters?'

'That is correct.'

'And what did Mr Peters offer you to try and make you change your mind?'

'He offered me money, a lot of money, and private education abroad for my children, and shopping trips to Europe and America for my wife.'

There were gasps from around the stadium as each section of the crowd picked up what Chilomba was saying in their own language. 'I refused all Mr Peters' offers.'

'You mean bribes?'

Chilomba's face loomed big on the screens. He cocked an eyebrow and smiled knowingly. Faintly he nodded.

Angry shouts erupted around the stadium, fuelled by Joseph's masterpiece. Mo had discovered that Joseph had a flair for design. The images which had appeared on the big screens earlier were now being reinforced by leaflets handed out all around the stadium by Joseph and a few trusted friends. These showed photos of traumatised Zuzubians being escorted by armed guards away from their villages, and of empty buckets being shown at a dried up well, contrasting with a sprinkler flicking across an immaculate green on one of Garston Peters' golf courses. The photo of the malnourished boy shown earlier was placed opposite a table of six white guests in their finery enjoying a lavish and expensive meal.

Garston Peters was now desperate. He had to get to Godson Malembe and ask him to stop this. Kicking VIP ankles as he scrambled out, he rushed down to Malembe's table. The Minister of Finance looked up at him benignly. Then he looked away and yawned loudly. Peters realised to his horror that he hadn't been recognised.

There was only one thing left. He must charge Shane Dunster and grab his microphone. What he would do after that he had no idea. As he turned away from Malembe's table, a large figure blocked his way. He turned to one side and another stepped in front of him. Every way Peters turned, he was blocked off by either Stanley or Jake. It was now too late. The next round of the food eating competition was about to begin. Nineteen of the top food eaters from around the world were standing in readiness. The twentieth was not standing because he couldn't. Godson Malembe had just told those around him that he wished to take a snooze. Kirsten melted into the background, her mission accomplished.

The remaining contestants were true professionals. They knew each other well, for they met regularly at similar competitions around the world, especially within the USA. All but one were Americans, and the majority were enormous ex-prison guards and night club bouncers, their bellies hanging down far below their belts. Most of them had professional pseudonyms, like Hollow Legs Joe, Modest Jim Tucker and Gorgeous Gorging George. But two contestants stood out: a short, stocky but muscular Chinese man with a head band and dyed red hair; and the only lady competitor, an American of Indonesian parentage called Rose. She was so small that her head barely reached the shoulders of the contestants on either side of her, and remarkably she was slender.

The food before them was a seemingly limitless supply of McRory's hot dogs. The rules of this round were simple. The contestants had twelve minutes in which to eat as many hot dogs as they could. The top fourteen contestants who ate the most would go through to the final.

'Look at them ripping into their snorkers. I don't blame them, they look delicious. Wouldn't mind one or two of them myself. But I think I'll leave the heavy stuff to the experts.' Shane was bouncing about in the middle of the pitch, screaming encouragement until the round was over. 'That was a toughie. Five of our visiting competitors have been eliminated. That leaves fourteen for the Grand Final. While we wait for that, this is the time to ask you what you think of this event.' It was well into the afternoon, and Shane knew that only a tiny proportion of the crowd would have been able to afford to visit the vending stalls. McRory's rules had forbidden any other food or drink to be brought into the stadium, so nearly the whole crowd was famished and thirsty.

'Well, you've been watching these people stuff themselves. How do you feel about it?' Again he spoke in three languages. 'Is a food eating competition a good thing for Zuzubia? Is it fair that you have to sit and watch a few people who have too much food when you have too little? Don't you think it's only fair that you should be allowed to share some of the food?' Murmurs became groans which grew to a cacophony of dissent. 'Well, good and patient people of Zuzubia, I've got news for you. Thanks to the generosity of Mr Garston Peters, there will be lots of food for all. Mr Peters has decreed that all the food that's left over at the end, and he's assured me there'll be plenty of that, will be shared out amongst you before you leave.'

There were roars of approval. In the VIP stand, McRory went ape. He lunged at Peters, one hand grabbing the lapel of his jacket and the other stabbing at his chest. 'I told you, no handouts, you lump of cowclap. It's in the fecking contract. All the fecking food belongs to me before, during and after the contest.'

'It's not me,' wailed Peters, 'It's Dunster. He's done this.'

'Don't you come the rubber pig with me, you heap of scutter.'

Peters curled himself up like a submissive dog.

Shane was speaking again. 'And now I want to introduce you to a lovely lady who can make sauces like no one else in the world. This is Mama Kuli, and these are her sauces.'

Peters extricated himself from McRory's clinch just sufficiently to be able to peer over his shoulder at one of the screens, now displaying his prototype bottles of Mama Kuli's sauces.

McRory slammed Peters against a wall. 'Those aren't my products, you fecking bastard.'

'But they're going to be,' wailed Peters.

'Not now they're not, you fecking eejit.'

'Mama Kuli,' asked Shane in Obooboan, 'you made these sauces, right?' Mama Kuli smiled proudly. 'And what is Mr Garston Peters doing with them?'

'He steal them,' she squeaked. 'He take them. They're mine, but he take them.'

'And did he give you any money for them?'

'No money, he steal.'

Shane repeated the conversation in Swahili. Rioting had started over on the far side of the stadium where Mama Kuli's family and supporters were grouped. Police were starting to run round the ground.

'Thank you, Mama Kuli. Another example of the good work of an honest Zuzubian being stolen. Do you think that is right?' A huge chorus of 'No' roared back at him in three languages.

Black clouds were amassing in the East. Distant thunder was almost continuous.

'Right, sounds like someone's telling us to get a move on. Fourteen contestants left, and this is the final. This is the round which will decide who's going to be crowned the Food Eating Champion of Zuzubia. Before them they each see a large plate. On that plate are five whole *Cheapie Chicken* breasts. That's not all. Also on the plate is half a kilo of *Chips on Fire*. Now that might not seem that much. But remember, these guys have been cramming tucker into their faces since eleven o'clock this morning. And those *Chips on Fire*, man, they're hot. H.O.T. It won't be easy. But it's a straight dash to the line now. The first contestant to show a clean plate will be the winner. Are you ready, contestants? Go!'

Diminutive Rose grabbed a chicken breast and tore it in half with the finality of someone despatching an unwanted letter from a ditched lover. She pushed each one into her mouth, masticating like a demented squirrel. Her hands went up and down to her mouth in a robotic rhythm, her left with food, her right with cups of water from which she took lightning but tiny sips. In no time she'd demolished all five chicken breasts. To either side of her, two pot-bellied giants were slurping, dribbling, and nodding as they tried to put more than just their jaws into the effort of chewing. Beyond one of them, the Chinese man with the red hair and the headband showed a smoother technique, but he looked to be way behind Rose. She had a greedy confidence about her, in contrast to her rivals' dogged struggles. Now she turned to the *Chips on Fire*. Screwing her eyes against the heat, she ignored the water and used both hands to rhythmically cram her mouth. The pouches of her cheeks bulged like a hamster's, but the chips kept disappearing.

Kirsten looked along the line of tables. As far as she could tell, all the other contestants still had one or more chicken breasts and most of their chips still to eat. By the time she looked back, Rose was leaping about, arms above her head. She'd won by a distance.

A man ran up to Shane in the middle of the pitch with a piece of paper.

'We have a winner. You little ripper! The winner of the food eating competition is.' Shane paused for effect. 'Rose Ross. Good onya, Rose. You've ripped the hell out of the lot of them.'

Then, for the first time, Shane fell silent. He stood with head bowed, then theatrically spun round on his heels and slowly raised his eyes to one of the big screens. Instead of McRory's *Cheapie Chickens* and *Chips on Fire,* there was a photo of two rival products, *Clumber Carvery* and *Chips We Love*.

McRory was already at Peters' throat by the time Shane bellowed in Obooboan to the ladies of a large township five miles south of Kumbala, 'Ladies, now strip!'

Approximately two hundred women, who'd been bussed in by Shane, stood up and removed their dresses, exposing tee-shirts with the words, '*Cheapie Chickens* are shit', with the word 'shit' in three languages. The effect was only slightly diminished by a significant number of ladies over-enthusiastically removing their tee-shirts as well, revealing that nothing was written on their bare breasts.

So long as McRory was attacking Peters, there was no need for Stanley and Jake to box him in, so they stood back, leaving McRory to do more than just contain Peters.

'I'll clatter your bangers, you jibber. You're bucked, Peters, you farteen.' McRory had him by both lapels and seemed to be shouting through him rather than at him. 'I'm going to break the lard out of your taws.'

'It wasn't me,' squealed Peters. 'I haven't done any of this.'

McRory had lifted Peters off the ground and was turning as though looking for a suitable patch to slam him into the ground. 'You're a no user, Peters, I'm going to banjax your kaks.' He suddenly let go and Peters only just kept his balance. 'Just let me plant one on your gob that'll take you within an ass's roar of your life, you gazooney.'

By pausing if only for a second to assess his target, McRory allowed Peters to make his escape. Realising once more that the microphone was the key to everything, he dodged past first McRory then Stanley, then Jake, and leapt down the steps two at a time.

Four figures were pounding across the turf towards Shane: Peters in the lead followed by McRory, followed closely behind by a sprinting Jake, followed at a distance by a puffing Stanley.

Shane saw Peters coming and neatly stepped aside. A confused Peters ran on past, lost sight of him and paused, trying to reassess his bearings. McRory, like the international prop forward he'd once been, slammed into Shane knocking him sprawling. He seized the microphone. 'You're a fierce hoor at business, Peters, you fecking wanker, you're in breach of your contract so many times that you won't have enough orifices to stick all my writs in. You're finished, you gobeen, I'll see to that.'

To Jake and Stanley watching at close quarters, it seemed that Peters had at last gained some courage. In fact it was the lure of the microphone. With desperate recklessness, he offered himself within range of McRory once more as he tried to seize the mic.

The undignified sight of two businessmen brawling in front of cameras, a microphone and twenty-five thousand people appealed to Jake's sense of the absurd so much that he felt the urge to participate. Seeing McRory was having difficulty shouting into the microphone while physically laying into Peters, Jake boldly stepped between them and seized the mic. 'Break! I said Break!' McRory and Peters did indeed break off to stare at Jake in astonishment. 'Now, I want a clean fight, no gouging, no kidney punching, ear nibbling, head butting or hitting below the belt. Right, box on!' Jake was dancing up and down still clutching the mic, urging them on. 'Go on, hit me with your handbag. Here's one I made earlier, kerflop!'

Perhaps it was the memory of that night when Peters had dined at *Waters of Eostre* and Jake had been insufferably rude. Perhaps it was the memory of Jake's face thrust up at him and impertinently questioning the fact that Tangle had served Peters with different food to the rest of them. Or perhaps it was Peters' innate cowardice that made him fight back at a weaker target than the ox-like McRory. Whatever the reason, it was Jake whom Peters took a swing at rather than McRory. Jake partly turned away, Peters' fist catching him on the shoulder, spinning him round so that he lost his balance.

Stanley, who had at last caught up with the others, saw red in a way he hadn't experienced since the days when he'd been an avid watcher of *Downsiders*. With the image of big Kev of *Downsiders* before him (in reality himself, heroic Stanley), he set out to avenge the injury done to his ally and best mate Jake. He took a huge swing at Peters from behind. Peters went down in a sort of balletic spiralling twirl, like a high-speed auger entering the turf.

As Stanley straightened, rubbing his hands partly in satisfaction and partly in pain, an unstoppable tide overwhelmed them. Stanley, the fallen Peters, McRory, Shane and Jake were all trampled under a galloping stampede of Zuzubians pouring out of the stands, aiming for the kitchen and food store.

Jake, lying on the turf for the second time in less than a minute, looked up to see what looked like a hundred bare breasts swinging and silently clanging past him, and then they were gone.

For the last time, the two huge screens lit up. A head and shoulders picture of Garston Peters with an extremely unflattering expression seemed to be watching everyone. He looked sly, devious and venal. Beneath his portrait were the words 'Totally responsible' in English, Swahili and Obooboan.

Three minutes later, the sky burst asunder, all the electrics went out, people screamed, and the event was washed to an end in a riot of gorging spectators, mud and confused police, who didn't know who the villains were, but wielded their batons just in case.

No one noticed two people near the rostrum, tears of laughter and rainwater spilling down their faces. Mo and Kirsten, hands aloft, were high-fiving.

CHAPTER FIFTEEN

Odile, still devastated by Rutt's cruel rebuttal, had returned to breakfasting late and alone. Kwame, of a different mind, had not given up. Each morning his loins were stirred by the sight of Madam so well-resourced. It excited him to think that he was playing a key part in maintaining her voluptuousness. He hadn't forgotten the stinging slap to his face, but the more he looked back to the incident the more stimulated he was by it. He had, he told himself, merely pushed his attentions on her too fast. Like a female elephant in the early stages of *oestrus*, she'd indicated that she was not quite ready. And the thrill of physical contact, even a flat-handed wallop, raised the tremendous probability that Madam was playing hard to get. For just a little longer he must control his *musth*. With that in mind, and body, Kwame whistled to himself as he prepared Madam's vast plate of food, ready for Chef to add the sausages, eggs, and sauces.

Odile tried to concentrate on the short-term. She'd decided she'd made a huge mistake in coming to Africa. Why had she come? For sunshine? There wasn't any; the rain was relentless. To see the animals? Yes, she'd seen some deer and giraffes and some piggy things, but that was a week ago. The roads were so treacherous that all safaris had been cancelled for this week. She still hadn't seen a lion. As for company, well there wasn't any, at least open to her. Rutt's offensiveness now meant that she couldn't face Teeny or Chest. That peculiar man McRory seemed to spend his days either in his room or going through paperwork in the lounge. If anyone spoke to him he did little more than grunt. Anyhow, he'd gone now, back to Ireland or wherever he came from. A group of Japanese, at least that's what she thought they were, had simply smiled at her when she'd tried to make conversation, and now they'd left too. That arty woman, what was her name, Lola, was voluble enough, but she said such peculiar things that Odile never knew what she was on about. That left the tall, distinguished gentleman, Granville Summers. Now he was someone she fancied, once she'd got Rutt out of her system. But when she'd tried to engage him in conversation, it had been something of a disaster.

'Do you mind if I ask you something, Doctor?'

'I'm not a doctor,' Granville replied severely.

'Oh dear, I'm so sorry, they told me...'

'I'm a retired surgeon. Retired. Surgeons are addressed as Mr.'

'I see.' (Odile didn't.) 'Well, Mr...'

'You can call me Granville. I'm on holiday.' He

said that to make sure Odile didn't start asking any medical questions. It didn't work.

'I've been suffering a lot recently.'

Granville sighed loudly. 'What have you been suffering from?' His voice dripped with disdain in a tone which said, go on, tell me if you must.

'It's my Simpsons.'

'Your what?'

'My Simpsons.' Odile wondered whether his apparent ignorance of a perfectly good medical term was confirmation that he wasn't a proper doctor.

'Do you mean your symptoms?'

'Oh silly me. Yes, I do think that's it. My symptoms.'

'Well, what symptoms have you got?'

'They're awfully sore.'

'Your symptoms are sore. Your symptoms are sore.' Odile wondered whether the unquestioning repetition meant that he didn't believe her or whether he was floundering, in which case he definitely was a complete fraud. 'Would you like to tell me where your symptoms are?'

'They're down there.'

Granville had retired six years ago. He was experienced enough to know that when a female patient said 'down there,' it spelt trouble. He decided to call her bluff. 'Would you like to show me?'

This presented a problem for Odile. The pain was in her feet, but it was impossible for her to get to them or even see them. 'They're at the bottom.'

'Your bottom?'

'The bottoms of my feet.'

'Ah. You mean the soles?'

'I think so. Someone told me I should take St John's Wort. Do you think that's right?'

The pause was so long that Odile wondered if this man knew anything. He must be a complete quack not to have heard of St John's Wort.

'St John's Wort, for those who believe in such things, is a herbal remedy for the treatment of depression, anxiety and insomnia. Are you suffering from any of those things?'

'All of them.'

'Let me get this straight. Your symptoms are in your feet, but you want a cure for depression, anxiety and sleep disorder?'

Odile was as confused as Granville. 'No, I mean sorry, it's my feet. Forget the others. I want St John's Wort for my feet.'

'Why would you want St John's Wort for your feet?'

Was he being awkward or just stupid? 'It's my warts. They're paining me.'

'Warts. St John's Wort for warts. Hm, I see.' Perhaps this woman really was crass enough to think they were connected. Perhaps St John, John the Baptist or John the Divine, had suffered from warts, discovered this herbal remedy, and given his name to the cure ever since. Intriguing hypothesis, and absolute balderdash.

'I've heard that homo-opathy is very good.'

Granville felt like saying that being gay wasn't a disease. Instead he replied, 'Homeopathy is a placebo dressed up in all its finery. Now look, I'm on holiday. I'm retired. I'm neither a GP nor a pharmacist, and I never was. Even if I were, I cannot prescribe medicines to you for all sorts of reasons.'

No, Granville Summers was no comfort or source of company either. The man was so aloof his head was through the ceiling. No, there was nothing for it. She'd made a huge mistake coming to Africa. All she could do was gain tiny pleasures from tiny moments, like when she would take the first mouthful of the breakfast which was due to appear any second now.

Kirsten sat very still, a hand clutching her stomach. She couldn't believe what she was reading on her screen. Her mind was in such turmoil that she was far from digesting the full implications. But the basic fact was clear: someone had hacked into Chuck Larter's computer.

'I'm very sorry, Kirsten. I don't know how this has happened. I had what I thought was a secure firewall, but they still got past it. The system didn't even detect it. The first I knew was when I Googled 'toad' and got 'scrotum toad' several times. Every detail you'd sent me and more besides is on the Web for all to see. It seems they've picked up all my search history on the subject too. It's all there, I'm afraid, you can see it for yourself: location, the known history of the toad, even a biography of you. Goddammit, there's even instructions on how to get to *Waters of Eostre*. I just can't think what to say to you, Kirsten. Apologies seem so inadequate. You trusted me as the one guy to keep your secret and I let you down.

'It'll be small comfort after that, but I do have a piece of good news, if you can take it from me, Kirsten. The DNA test showed that your *Bufo Sayeri* isn't that close to *Bufo Regularis* and it isn't a *Xenopus* either. In fact it has characteristics which justify that abused and over-used word unique.

'How can I end this? Simply by saying that I'm very, very sorry, Kirsten, and if you can think of a way I can make amends, please do let me know.'

Kirsten told them all over dinner. Tangle had been the one she'd been dreading. She was so protective of her own special ideal of tranquillity that the thought of hundreds of people trampling over her beloved paradise - scientists, journalists and sightseers - would traumatise her.

But she reacted calmly. 'Put it this way,' she said in her deliberate way, 'a week ago I was going to be thrown out of *Waters of Eostre*. Thanks to you Kirsten, and you Mo, and you Jake and you Stanley, well, you've saved me. How could I possibly be angry? I'm grateful. How can it be your fault, Kirsten, that you've made a great discovery? And how could anyone blame you for what happened to someone else's computer the other side of the world?'

There were tears and hugs, and facetious comments from Jake. Mo summed it up nicely, 'We make quite a team. But we need to prepare ourselves for the invasion. It will come.'

Odile was torturing herself by counting down the seconds to when Kwame would emerge from the kitchen with her breakfast. Five, four, three, two, one, zero... no. Eight, seven, six, five, four, three, two, one, zero. It must be soon. She was salivating furiously. Please let it be this time. Eleven, ten, nine, eight, seven, six... There was a wrenching sound the like of which she'd only heard once before, on a cruise ship in a storm. A chandelier crashed down onto the table in front of her. Odile screamed. A prolonged roar to her right accompanied the sight of the windows over the river shattering ahead of her. Suddenly the whole room lurched. The kitchen doors burst open to reveal a terrifying void. Cookers, fridges, worktables and people had disappeared.

The only sound was the roaring of the river and a rumbling as an armchair came sliding into the dining room from the lounge. Odile, by now on the floor, was hit in the back. Somehow, with an agility which would have astonished anyone had they been watching, she heaved herself upwards in an effort to prevent herself from being swept into the river. The effect was that the armchair gathered her up as it continued its slide. So tightly was Odile wedged between the arms that the force of hitting the water failed to dislodge her. She and her mount, pounded on all sides, took off downstream at a terrifying rate.

Huge trees slammed into elegant tables, and wooden bowls bobbed excitedly among the bodies of dead animals, all hurtling down the river at the speed of a cruising car.

Kwame, the sole survivor from the kitchen, entered the water clinging to a butcher's block. As he sped down the river he looked back in horror at the rapidly diminishing remains of the hotel. Water was everywhere and with it the flotsam of the greatest flood Zuzubia had ever known, together with half the fabric of *Crowned Crane Lodge*.

Spinning on his butcher's block, Kwame thought he noticed something downstream ahead of him which took what little remained of his breath away. There, in midstream, he thought he'd seen, yes there, definitely, unmistakably, Madam apparently sitting in the water and seemingly calling to him. He could see her jaw working and her arms waving, but he couldn't hear her above the din. The look of supplication on her face would haunt him for the rest of his life.

Gradually the butcher's block turned less crazily in the water and Kwame could no longer see her. It hit a tree trunk whose base had wedged into the bank. He was almost thrown off but just managed to cling on. The butcher's block and he were directed shorewards. He flung himself onto the tree trunk and scrambled along it to the bank. He lay there panting then clambered to his feet. Madam! He looked up and thought he could see her, but she was a long way downstream and he couldn't be sure. It might be a hippo. He staggered along the bank which wasn't really a bank, but an extension of the river. Several times the force of the water knocked him off his feet. He was in great danger of being swept into the main current again. Still he floundered on, at times having to swim because the water was so deep. When he arrived opposite the place where he'd thought he'd seen her, he found a lone bull elephant but no sign of Madam. Tearful and shivering, he turned slowly back towards the remains of the hotel, by now several miles upstream.

CHAPTER SIXTEEN

They couldn't make up their minds at *Waters of Eostre*. Was an invasion imminent or not? Were hordes of photographers, hacks and sightseers even now moving through the darkness, all drawn by the lure of the toad? Or was a greater force, which had sinisterly revealed itself over the past ten hours or so, preventing them?

Tangle was insistent. 'It's very kind of you to offer to move out, Kirsten. Maybe it would stop these people coming to *Waters of Eostre* or some of them at least. But we stick together. And look now, where would you go?'

'I do not know. Maybe I would find somewhere.'

'There you are then, you don't know!'

'I cannot believe I am among such lovely people.' The men, used to Tangle's occasional tears, were embarrassed by even slight signs of emotion coming from Kirsten.

Mo, practical as ever, suggested they plan for people arriving. 'We may get several types: those who contact us first, those who just turn up at the door, and those who try to get in round the back. They may be media, politicians, scientists or just people who want to get a look at the celebrity.'

'That's the toad, Kirsten, not you.'

Mo flicked his head disapprovingly at Jake. 'But we're overlooking something. No one's contacted us. Why? Because they can't. All communications are down, have been since this morning. Right, Tangle?'

'Phone, computer, nothing at all. It's a miracle we've got electrics.'

'I can't get a line either,' said Kirsten.

'I think we know the reason, don't we?' Mo looked at them all in turn.

'Have you seen it?' Stanley rarely entered into debates, so everyone turned to him surprised. 'I looked down from the rock this afternoon. It's like a kettle boiling. The flat land is covered with water as far as I could see. I saw lots of nasty things floating past.'

'Not condoms?'

'Please be quiet, Jake,' Tangle snapped. 'What sort of things did you see, Stanley?'

'I saw dead bodies.'

Jake was excited by that. 'Dead bodies?'

'Animals, big ones, lots of them.'

'I didn't see that,' said Kirsten, 'but I did see the river was in full flood and it had burst over the banks. The whole area for kilometres around is under water, and there are boiling rapids, like Stanley says.'

Mo got up and walked to the door. He opened it

and looked meaningfully back at the others. The roar from the river was apocalyptic. He closed the door. 'So yes, we can plan for invasion, but if you think about it we've got protection on three sides. No one's going to be crossing the river. So all we need is some extra security to the west. But is that really our priority? Those floodwaters stretch for miles in all directions except where the land is high. We know that it's flat for, what, twenty, thirty miles from here towards Kumbala? No one's going to get here for a long time.'

'I wish we knew what was happening out there.' Tangle looked depressed.

'What about the radio?' Stanley asked.

'I will not have radio here.' Tangle was stubborn. 'Nor television.'

Jake tutted. 'All that turbulent water. We should check which way it's spiralling.'

Mo shot him a glance like a poisoned dart. It was a code of conduct between them that they should be respectful of Tangle's eccentricities in front of her. Jake looked contrite. Mo smiled at him to make up. 'Come on, look on the bright side. No road, no unwanted visitors. No communications, no appointments.'

'That's a relief. My diary's full already.'

This time Mo grinned at Jake. Kirsten said goodnight and left for her house. The others sat for a while and talked about what her life would be like over the next few weeks.

'It's such a big thing, that toad,' said Mo. 'It's not as though she's discovered, rediscovered, some tiny insect. And it's an extraordinary looking thing.'

'Especially when you look underneath.' Tangle looked embarrassed the moment she'd said it.

There was a loud and urgent knocking on the door. Stanley, who was nearest and liked to do such things, went to answer it. They heard voices, and then Stanley returned. 'The invasion has started. I told them to go away.'

'Thank you, Stanley.' Tangle looked pleased then troubled. 'Where will they go? I don't want them camping.'

'I bolted the door.'

The banging started even louder and more insistent.

'I'll go.' Jake unbolted the door.

'How dare they?' Tangle looked affronted.

'Toad Hall? Not here, gone away, poop-poop! Come back another day, preferably next year. Invasions by appointment only.'

'Please! Please!' The wailing female voice was so insistent that the others jumped to their feet. Standing next to Jake, they peered into the darkness. A group of bedraggled people were huddled outside. A tall, elderly man, dignified in spite of torn clothes and blood on his chin, stepped forward.

'We've had a disaster. One of our party is injured. Several of those we were with are dead. May we come in please?'

Next morning at breakfast they told their story. The tall Englishman did much of the talking, punctuated now and then by the others: two American men, an

American woman and another woman who looked Mediterranean or possibly Middle Eastern.

'We were staying upriver. There's been a lot of rain over the past month. We've been on holiday and hadn't been able to get out as often as we'd have liked. Then today, at nine-thirty,' Granville Summers paused. 'It seems longer.'

'A lifetime,' said Lola.

'What must have been a flash flood of extraordinary power knocked a large part of the hotel into the river. We don't know exactly what hit it, but it must have been more than just water. Rocks, tree trunks and even dead animals were seen.'

'I saw them.'

'You did, Stanley,' said Mo soothingly.

'Where was this?' asked Tangle.

'*Crowned Crane Lodge*. Do you know it?'

'I've been there.'

'We know for certain that between seven and nine people died, maybe several more. Odile was having breakfast...'

Teeny started sobbing.

'The dining room and kitchen simply disappeared into the river. We think a waiter died and one or two kitchen staff. There was a meeting room which also went. The Manager was talking to either three or four of his senior staff. All perished. Two men appeared shortly afterwards looking fit and well, but they disappeared a few minutes later and we never saw them again. We simply don't know how many other staff were around when the building went or what happened to them. We have one casualty, as you can see. Poor Chest here was caught by a falling pillar which pinned him down by his left leg. It's broken in two places, though not as badly as I'd first feared.'

'On the mend,' said a voice from the floor.

'Oh Chest!' Teeny started crying again.

'He's magnificent,' said Chest. 'Granville's a surgeon, retired, but boy did he deliver. The very best. Deserves a movie to be made about him. Make a note of that, Honey.'

Granville took the compliment with a stately nod. 'It didn't take long to realise that we had to get out. Half of the hotel had gone, there was no food and more importantly no water, at least that we could trust. We knew we had to move fast. Being out in a game park on foot by day is one thing, but by night...' Granville shook his head. 'Once I'd set Chest's leg and Rutt here had cobbled together a stretcher, we were ready to go.'

Lola turned from Granville to the others. 'He's been magnificent. Without him...' Teeny started sobbing again.

Granville continued. 'We looked at a map and saw that the nearest settlement was here. We knew we shouldn't follow the river for all sorts of reasons: flooding, greater danger of being cornered by animals, greater distance due to bends in the river. We could see a track, at least that's what we thought it was, heading more or less directly to here, so we decided to go for that. We set out just after mid-day. We had no food, no water, no weapons and no medicines. All we had to carry was Chest.'

'Sorry to be a burden.'

'His left fibula has a transverse fracture four inches above the calcaneus.'

'That's a snappy description.'

'Jake is our resident fool here,' said Mo. 'In the Shakespearean sense, of course. You'll quickly learn to ignore him.'

Granville closed his eyes and opened them again. 'Also, there's a comminuted fracture of the cuboid.'

'Apart from that, I'm fine,' roared Chest.

'Take it easy, Sugar Cake.' Chest and Teeny smiled lovingly at each other.

'We knew we were in trouble soon after leaving the hotel. The track plunged into goodness knows how many feet of water. The whole area was one huge lake. The only hope was some high ground a mile or so to the north, so we retraced our steps and headed for that. Long before we got to it, we were faced with a huge herd of buffalo. There must have been at least sixty of them.'

'Easily,' said Teeny.

'There were five of us. If we'd all been fit and upright we might have got away with advancing on them line abreast, and they'd probably have moved off. But two of us had to carry Chest, and we reasoned that we weren't imposing enough to be certain of scaring them off. So we had to head off north-east, in almost the wrong direction.'

'Tell them about the rhino.' Teeny's eyes glistened.

'That came later. We hadn't spotted him behind a bush. He came snorting out and stood there staring at us. Then he started trotting towards us. We got behind a tree, but Lola, with incredible bravery, came out waving her arms and diverted the brute.'

'She's a real heroine. She should get a medal.' Chest turned from Lola to Teeny. 'Another one for a movie, Candyflops.'

What no one said until Granville confided in Mo much later was that Teeny had been screaming, 'Do something, Rutt! Save us like you did in *Facing the Onslaught*.' The ensuing argument behind the tree had attracted the attention of the rhino still further until Lola had intervened. Rutt's contribution had been, 'I can't! I can't!' Granville's own had been, 'He's an actor and that was a film, you stupid woman!'

Granville finished his story of how, as darkness fell, they thought they were lost, their terror at the animal noises around them, their relief at seeing the lights of *Waters of Eostre* above them, their difficulty in finding a way up the rock in the dark, and their constant slipping in the mud, fearing that Chest might slide off his stretcher at any minute. At the end, Granville asked Tangle if he might have a word in private. She motioned him into her office.

'Trumper needs medical attention. I've set his leg, but there's a danger of infection from the wound. Also he needs an x-ray and almost certainly an operation to reset his leg. We need to get him to hospital as soon as possible.'

Tangle gazed out of the window. 'The road to Kumbala will be flooded, I'm sure of that. We have no communication with the outside world. No landline, no internet, no phone. We don't have radio or TV here.'

'What medical supplies have you got?'

'The usual. Bandages, pain killers, antiseptic ointment, plasters, cough mixture, not much else.'

'Antibiotics?'

'No.'

Granville bit his lip and nodded slowly. 'Getting help must be our priority. Let's join the others.'

They made a quick plan. Jake was to drive the van as far as he could along the Kumbala road and report back. Stanley would go with him. Mo and Rutt would walk round the rock surveying the land in all directions, or rather the land and water. Tangle wanted to go with Kirsten to find the African workers and speak to them, but she was needed at the house, so Granville would accompany Kirsten. The priority at the house was to make an inventory of all supplies, especially food, and this was something only Tangle could do. Lola would help her. Teeny would stay with Chest.

Jake and Stanley soon returned. They'd got less than a mile before they'd had to turn back. Mo reported a grim picture from up on the rock. There was water as far as the eye could see to the south and east. To the north there were floods for a couple of miles or so until the land rose gradually up to some low hills. But as the residents of *Waters of Eostre* knew, in that direction lay wilderness. Their view to the west had been blocked by forest, but it was unlikely to be flooded up there, as the ground was mostly high. They knew that a track, barely passable in a vehicle even in the dry season, and certainly not in Tangle's old van, led to a hill a couple of miles away. There were Obooboan settlements up there, beyond the village where Tangle's African workers lived. Further still, the map showed a road, and it did head south towards Kumbala and civilisation. But it was a good twelve miles away, and in any case they could see on the map that it gradually bent east and joined the other road only about six miles to the south of *Waters of Eostre*, just a mile from the river. Both Jake and Mo thought they knew where the roads met, and the land there, they said, was low lying. They were trapped.

Tangle reported on her inventory. 'With ten of us to feed we'll soon run out of basics. But look, we've got all those fresh fruit and vegetables in the gardens. There's plenty of carbohydrate in the root vegetables and we can always make flour from cassava. If anyone wants meat they can go hunting for it, I mean literally.'

'There's definitely no way of using a mobile phone here?' asked Granville. 'Lola, Teeny and Rutt had them at *Crowned Crane Lodge*, but they've been lost in the disaster.'

'Anyhow,' said Mo, 'there won't be a signal. No one uses them here.'

'There was a man here last year.' Tangle showed more disgust than enthusiasm. 'He said that if you walked up that hill to the west you could just get a faint signal sometimes. He had one.'

Mo knocked the idea on the head. 'The fact remains, no one here has a cell phone.'

'I've got one.' Everyone except Stanley and of course Chest jumped in their seats and turned to stare at Kirsten. 'I didn't think I could use it here. It will need charging of course.'

Jake leaned across and kissed her on the cheek before she could take evasive action. 'First a toad and then a phone. Any more rediscoveries up your sleeve, my little Danish pastry? Perhaps a new type of dinosaur lurking in the bush?'

'I thought they were extinct,' she glared at him, 'until I met you.'

CHAPTER SEVENTEEN

Jake was giving a lesson in the practicalities of life at *Waters of Eostre*. 'Our ethos is that nothing must be wasted. Everything must be sustainable. We shun fossil fuels.' Teeny looked interested, Lola suspicious, Chest disgusted. The words 'ethos' and 'sustainable' were anathema to him, and anyone who talked about shunning fossil fuels was a dangerous liberal.

Jake was oblivious. 'Tangle is very strict. She's from Wales.'

Teeny wondered what that meant. Had Tangle worked with the creatures in a previous career?

'I happen to know the answer to that one, Sweetie Bunch. Wales is a small and unimportant state in England.'

It took Jake a moment to recover sufficiently to be able to continue. 'Our electricity is generated by a windmill.'

Lola was dismissive. 'I thought there wasn't much wind in this part of Africa.'

'Ah, you see, no, that is why we have a wood burner to power the blades and make them turn.'

Lola saw through that one too. 'Wood is not sustainable, at least not the sort that grows around here.'

'Ah, yes, quite right, which is why we don't actually use the wood burner directly. Not for burning wood, I mean. Tangle has linked it to the toilets. It's the toilets which provide the power.'

'Methane?' Lola was thinking of her rats in the London sewers.

'No.'

'Heat, the rotting process? Composting?'

'No, you'll never guess.'

'What, then?'

'Gravity.'

'From the toilets?'

'That's right. We've created a hundred and forty foot drop directly below.'

'What d'ya do that for?' It wasn't that Chest didn't believe Jake, it was simply that he hated this do-goodin' bullshit.

'For the turds. They hurtle through the air and land on a series of blades which, when they turn, power the wood burner, except that it isn't a wood burner any more, it's merely an intermediary conveyor of power to turn the sails of the windmill. Ingenious, eh?'

'I get it,' roared Chest. 'So finally the windmill generates the electricity! Well darn me! What a waste of time and, would you believe it, energy.'

Jake held up a hand. 'Not quite. The windmill

has mirrors which flash in the sunlight as the blades turn.'

'Let me guess, these are picked up by photoelectric cells. And it's those that power the lights!'

'No. The lights shine into the eyes of two donkeys who walk forward to avoid the flashing. They turn a wheel which generates the electricity. It's all very ecological, you see.'

'I love donkeys,' said Teeny. 'Can we go and see them now?'

Lola did a slow handclap. 'Very amusing, Jake.'

'Tangle insists that we each pull our weight by making some specialist contribution. I, for instance, am studying the ways of the virginal thrush.' There was a long pause, filled only by a smirk from Lola.

Teeny thought the bird sounded vaguely familiar. 'Is it called the virginal thrush because it still hasn't found a mister thrush?' she tittered coyly.

'Sounds like it's found a few too many,' snapped Lola.

'Naturally, we recycle all our waste products here. Before they fall a hundred and forty feet, the solids are separated from the liquids. The liquids are then filtered - at least I assume they are; hm, I've never really checked - to provide our drinking water.'

The word recycling alone was bound to get Chest going again. 'You mean we're drinking our own piss?'

'Not just your own. Be fair, other people's too.'

Teeny looked alarmed. 'Aren't there any side effects?'

'Oh loads. And front effects, and rear effects.'

Lola shook her head at Teeny pityingly. Could she really be lapping up this shit? An apt way of putting it, she thought grimly to herself.

'By the way,' said Jake, 'that reminds me. If you are ill as a result, do please make sure you vomit into the recycling bowl. Tangle insists that we compost everything here.'

Chest wasn't having that. 'I'm telling you, Sweetums, you don't have to do that, not while I'm around and kicking. Well, partly kicking. It's all phoney baloney, this ecology nonsense. What I want to know is what this mysterious animal is that I overheard a couple of your colleagues talking about. With my busted leg it'll be a while before I can go huntin' again. But I sure am curious to know what that beast might be.'

'Ah, you mean Kirsten's great discovery. I'm not sure I ought to be talking about that. You see... All right, then.' Jake moved his chair closer to Chest and assumed a loud stage whisper. 'It's an animal which everyone thought was extinct. She's rediscovered it.'

'Is it big?'

'A fair size. Let's say you wouldn't want to meet it on a narrow path on a dark night.'

'My God!' Chest's blazing eyes revealed how impressed he was. 'Are you able to tell me what it is?'

'Sorry.'

'Just a hint, maybe?'

'Put it this way, if you were to have a guess and were on the right lines, I wouldn't put you off the scent.'

'Let me see now. There's the white tiger. I've heard they're so rare that no one's actually seen one for a while outside a zoo.'

Jake leaned back in his chair with a sphinx-like smile.

'No!' Chest didn't dare believe it. Had he really got it in one?

Jake winked.

'Well I'll be darned!'

'Keep it to yourself. Yourselves.' Jake sounded panicky, as though regretting he'd said too much. 'We don't want to be letting the cat out of the bag. The cat?'

Chest leaned back. 'Don't you worry, son. I've been producing movies for thirty years.'

'Thirty-two.'

'Thank you, Dream Girl, thirty-two years booking stars, planning locations, hiring directors. That requires heapsa confidentiality. Discretion is my middle name. Your secret's safe with me, and with Teeny. She's been by my side for all of that time and more...'

'Thirty-eight.'

'Is that right, my Cutesy Pie, well thirty-eight it is, so you can count on her too. And you, Lola?'

'Oh you bet,' said Lola acidly.

'Chest can't wait to get back hunting again,' gushed Teeny. 'It's why he came out to Africa, that and to plan his next movie.'

'We'll leave that subject for now,' said Chest sharply. He was still smarting over Rutt's rebuttal of his plan to shoot an African film about Gordy.

'And you Teeny?' Jake saw Teeny as a target for further leg pulling.

'Oh me, I came out to get a baby.'

'Do you know, for one moment I actually thought you said you came out here to get a baby.'

'I did.'

'To have a baby, how wonderful!'

'Oh, you flatterer!' Teeny shrieked with delight. 'I think I'm a bit old for that. No, I came out to buy one.'

'A baby? In the market?'

'I got him from a convent.'

'Ah I see. One of the nuns cheating on Jesus again.'

'I don't know what you mean, young man, and I don't think I want to.' Teeny had gone all huffy.

'She's chosen him to match her decor,' said Lola sourly.

Jake was loving this. 'You needn't have worried, Teeny. You know you can have him genetically modified to any colour you want. You still can.'

'Can I?'

'Yes, I especially recommend the various shades of blue genes.'

'Adopting a baby is a perfectly respectable thing to do,' said Chest sternly.

'Oh, I don't doubt it.' Jake sounded sincerely apologetic. 'When one can't have children of one's own it's the natural thing to do.'

'I've had children of my own.' Teeny's voice had thickened. 'I've lost touch with them. I disposed of them when they were teenagers. *Elegance Magazine* said that we women should have more 'me' time, so our children were one of the distractions I had to give up. My psychoanalyst backed me up. She told me I was doing the right thing; a brave and necessary sacrifice, she said.'

'Your psychoanalyst would say that.' Lola stared hard at Teeny, seeing only the frivolous socialite. 'The first task of therapists is to make sure their client really has a problem. If she has, they get her to talk about it in such a way as to make the problem worse. If their client hasn't got a problem, the analyst helps her manufacture one. If they're not sure, the task is to take something trivial and magnify it until it becomes an obsession. No one is allowed to leave a therapy session without being riddled with doubts and uncertainties. There must be no resolution at this stage; the bills aren't big enough. The client must be convinced that she's mentally unstable. Only then can the therapist start to lead her on the long path to a life contemplating her navel. If the patient shows signs of distress when addressing her problem, then full-on confrontation is prescribed to increase her anxiety. But if the patient seems ready to face up to reality, she's advised not to do so, but to work round it. That should take several more sessions. Whether the patient comes trembling before the source of her terror or creeps fearfully through the bushes of avoidance, the result is the same: fear, doubt and confusion, all cultivated by the shrink. Only then can the noble art of healing be applied. The patient is now well down a very long and expensive road.'

'Wow!' Jake was impressed. 'Creeping fearfully through the bushes of avoidance, eh?'

Teeny was less impressed. 'I thought you were my friend,' she snuffled, eyeing Lola out of the corners of her put-upon eyes, Princess Diana-style.

'There, there, my Cookie. I'm sure Lola didn't mean to.' Chest didn't know what Lola hadn't meant to.

Lola turned away, showing her profile in a statuesque way.

'What about you, Lola?' It sounded as though Jake was trying to keep the peace, although knowing him that was unlikely. 'Any children?'

Lola swung slowly back to face them. 'Not likely. The children are bad enough, but not as bad as the men that go with them. I was married to an Argentine once. Never again. Shouting, 'Take that!' every time he reached his climax was bad enough, but then he switched to 'Go-al!' every time he scored, so I sent him packing. That was the best part, getting rid of him.'

'Dump the grump,' offered Jake. 'Part with the fart, can the man, propella the fella.'

'You're a very rude young man,' Teeny sniffed. 'I was married to a Latino before I met my gorgeous Chest. He was a Catholic like me. He called me Impedimenta. Such a pretty name, don't you think?'

'This new baby of yours, boy or girl?' Jake asked.

'He's a boy. Benjamin.'

'You say you've bought him. Won't he be lonely, or do you plan to collect the whole set?'

'Oh he won't be lonely, we've got our darling little doggie called Witty the Fourth.'

'Teeny loves her doggie, don't you, Doll? She buys only the best silk for him to lie on, and when she goes on vacation she takes him to a hotel specially for dogs. He has his own room with TV and drinks cabinet and a private beach which can only be shared with a maximum of five other dogs.'

'Saves on the scooping.' Jake pretended to look approving. 'But don't you get just a teeny-weeny bit of conscience about his farts adding to global warming?'

'Oh don't get Chest started on global warming...'

She was too late. Chest had already launched himself. 'Those scientists make this baloney up so they can justify their existence. The more the polar ice cap melts, the more these concerned and caring worthies rush in to monitor it. They break up the ice with their ships, they breathe a lot of hot air, they piss on the snow so it melts some more, and then they say it's all man-made. That way they justify being paid to return so they can shit and piddle some more.'

'Just like Witty the Fourth,' Jake suggested.

Lola took over. Jake irritated her, she thought Chest was a boorish twat, but Teeny she despised with a passion. She recalled how Teeny had told her at *Crowned Crane Lodge* about her *soirées* and coffee mornings. She'd thought then what a vacuous life Teeny led, but even she had been too polite to say so at the time.

'Dogs are the ultimate parasite, skulking around the fringes of human existence, understanding next to nothing, wheedling favours from their mistresses. Only someone with the priorities of a socialite would indulge an animal like that.' Now she let rip. 'Is there anything more damning than to be considered a socialite? Actually there is: being one. A socialite has received not just an expensive education, but in most cases a good one. From it the socialite derives just two things: snobbery, when she has no justification whatsoever for elevating herself above her fellow human beings, most of whom achieve more than she does; and a consummate ability to adore the trivial, which she pursues relentlessly. She's an empty head who thinks people admire her for her charm, when in reality it's her money, earned by someone else. She fritters it on expensive baubles and designer clothes. People who buy and wear designer clothes are unable to cultivate their own individuality so they clutch at the identity of others, covering their intellectual nakedness by clothing themselves in celebrity-endorsed fashion items whose value to the pathetic creatures who wear them is the delusion that others respect them for their labels. So these feeble-minded victims of marketing bray and baa of a few brands find succour, when they should be embarrassed by their displays of craven conformity and financial waste. That's succour with an o, u, r, by the way. Sucker with a c, k, would be more appropriate.'

'The urge to splurge is endemic in the American female psyche,' said Jake impishly, 'but I don't know who you could be referring to, Lola.'

Lola hadn't finished. 'Look at me. I may be part of the flock with a sheep's brain to match, but I've got money which means I must be successful, and you'd better respect me for flaunting it, right? I'm worthless, talentless and if I had half a brain I'd get Graunchy or Ralph Polo or whoever to pay *me* to be a walking billboard, instead of paying money to be one for him. Don't tell me what to wear. I don't even tell myself. I get Karl or Ralph to do it for me.'

'You poor thing.' Teeny felt genuinely sorry for Lola and all her problems. It must be difficult being an artist with that funny temperament.

Tangle came up to them.

Teeny smiled at her enthusiastically. 'Jake's been telling us…'

Terrified of what the others might say, Jake leapt to his feet. 'Something you should know has just come up, Tangle. It's rather urgent. Will you excuse us?' He led a bewildered Tangle firmly by the arm, desperately trying to think up something to say to her.

CHAPTER EIGHTEEN

Rutt Revere was having serious doubts. Was God punishing him or testing him? Or had He abandoned him? Or was it the other way round? He'd come out to Africa to shoot lions and bears. Chest Trumper, who he'd thought was his bud, had only wanted to talk movies. But when Rutt had finally persuaded him that they should go huntin', the rain had prevented them even leaving the hotel. And then. And then. What was it God did to Noah? He sent a Great Flood because the world was made up of people who'd sinned, but He'd spared Noah because Noah was a Good Man. He'd spared Rutt, so surely Rutt too must have found favour in the sight of the Lord? This made him feel better.

There was more evidence. God had sent him on a great Exodus through the waters. No, that wasn't Noah, that was Moses. Rutt brooded over that and thought it didn't matter. Yeah, he'd parted the waters so the Chosen People might pass to a

Promised Land, and the waters had closed behind them again and confounded their enemies. There was just one problem. That hadn't happened. And who were the enemies? The buffalo? The rhino? And the last thing Rutt would describe this place as was the Promised Land. It didn't all stack up as it should.

Then Rutt realised a contradiction which knocked the bottom out of his Faith still further. Koota Hoki Sri Badabadanath wasn't a Christian, but he still believed in God. Which God? He preached that there was only one God who created the world yesterday. But according to the Bible, the Bible of Noah and Moses, the world was created, when was it, four thousand years ago. That was a hugely long time, surely far beyond what was possible? And Noah's flood, wasn't that a very long time ago too, perhaps three thousand years ago? But Rutt's flood was yesterday. God created the world yesterday. So perhaps Koota Hoki Sri Badabadanath was right after all? Everything was so complicated. He should stick to politics. At least the Tea Party made things simple.

Now God - one of them, whichever one - had sent Rutt a new temptation. His gonads were metaphorically aching through lack of action. It'd been two and a half weeks since he'd had a testicular release with that chick in Denver, and his loins were flexing for a performance now.

Rutt may have gotten religion, or two of them, but to the world he was still a Hollywood star. He was used to adulation and expected it. He wasn't getting any and that upset him. Teeny, of course, adored him. Chest had been narky towards him, but Chest was in the business, so he didn't count. Granville Summers was as oblivious to Rutt's status as that McRory man had been at *Crowned Crane Lodge*. Lola had come on to him at first. He'd quite fancied her, especially as babes were less than thin on the ground there. But when he'd knocked quietly on her bedroom door, she'd opened it with, 'Oh you! I thought you might try. Only a Brahman may enter this shrine. This lotus is foreclosed for sleep, perchance to dream. To you, my drooling Prince, goodnight.'

He hadn't a clue what she was on about and was not even sure what she'd said, but the way the door squashed his nose seemed flat out final. Ever since then she'd moved away whenever he'd come close, and somehow he no longer felt like attempting to melt her ice. Something to do with that walk yesterday. No more mystery. Too much of her had been revealed.

Now he was among a new set of people. What weirdos. Surely they must know who he was? That hoochie-koochie woman they called Tangle was acting as if she'd never heard of him. She was a true genitile, make no mistake. She talked in a spooky voice. Probably voodoo. The creakin' grandpa Stanley didn't seem to know anything. Doubt he's even heard of Jesus Christ or Marilyn Monroe. The Jew-boy Mo, oh yes, Rutt could tell that Mo recognised him, but he wasn't going to let on. No special treatment there. As for that dude Jake, every time he looked at Rutt he fluttered his eyebrows and put on an oafish grin. That left Kirsten. Danish, they say. She's a cool one. There's something about her. You might say she's kinda ordinary, but that's what makes her so foxy. Nothing out of place like. She's given me no clue she knows who I am, but I bet she does, and frankly it's giving me a hard on. Rutt imagined her making love. She would do it seriously, competently, silently. She would take the lead, then her neat little body would loosen and she'd melt for him, offering herself effortlessly, allowing him to command the pace. Then I'll throw her switch and have her yowling like a coyote in season. Jeez, I must stop this or I'll empty the trash without the bin. But I'll tell you this, my little Danish Lady. It won't be long before I go a-huntin', and it'll be a real pleasure, Ma'am.

Lola hadn't come out to Africa looking to get laid. She was still affected by the death of her mother. Her unexpected hormonal rush at finding herself in proximity to Rutt had been easily quelled once she'd cast her critic's eyes over him. To her his hunkiness was a shell enclosing a vacuum. No brain, no guts. He'd been pathetic with that rhino, squealing like a piglet. Leading man, my tush. He'd cowered at the back whimpering.

It had come as something of a shock to Lola to find that she was now smitten after all. The object of her fascination (and yes, it was just fascination she told herself) was someone whose movements thrilled her the more she watched them, like a piece of kinetic art which enthrals both through its simplicity and its changing complexity. Here was harmony, beauty and unpredictability. There was imperfection, sure, but that was all the more intriguing. The mannerisms were so distinctive, those hands so articulate, creative. Those dark shifting eyes, that slender slinkiness, a voice that was both expressive and musical, that eloquent hair which always seemed to lie carelessly across her breasts. Yes, Lola had become infatuated with Tangwystl Breeze. Lola was proud of her peerless appreciation of the body beautiful, be it male or female, and comfortable with blurring the boundaries between aesthetics and sexuality.

Had Tangle known this, she would have been highly alarmed. She was modest enough not to wish to be the subject of anybody's study, aesthetically or in any other way. There was nothing the slightest AC-DC about her. She had the object of her desire to contemplate, and that was Mo Guterman. She wasn't sure whether her feelings were reciprocated. There were times when Mo was gentle and attentive to her, and very occasionally she did think he looked at her in a certain pleasing way. But the only time she'd ever started to advance on him emotionally, he'd backed away and left the room. That had been when they were first sounding each other out on their respective views about Garston Peters. She hadn't dared show her feelings again because, as leader of a small, closed group, her whole world might fall apart if she made a wrong move. So she made none.

Of course Lola wasn't the only one to be fascinated by Tangle. Jake's passion for female

Welshness had brought him to *Waters of Eostre* in the first place. His shock at her age had lasted only days. The woman was so bleeding sexy with her dancing voice and silky movements, not forgetting those eyes and the way she twiddled her hair with her long bony fingers. Jake's desire for her, which he was incapable of expressing in a grown-up and joined-up way, was increasing by the week.

Tangle's inventory may have shown there was no need to ration food, but accommodation was a headache. Before the refugees had arrived there had been just enough places to sleep. In the main house Stanley, Jake and Tangle each had rooms to themselves upstairs. When Mo had arrived, Tangle had converted a downstairs storeroom into a fourth bedroom. Kirsten, not being a woofer, had her own house, most of which was filled with her equipment and specimens. Now Tangle had to find space for a further five people. Chest's injury meant that he had to sleep on the ground floor with Teeny in what had been Mo's room. Mo had to move upstairs and double up with Jake. Lola was forced to share with Tangle herself. That left one person to share with Stanley and one to move into Kirsten's house. Unfortunately there wasn't a female left, so Tangle chose the elderly and respectable Granville to sleep in Kirsten's house, not in her bedroom of course, but Kirsten would have to clear a space amongst her equipment somewhere. That left Rutt, who would have to double up with Stanley. Strange bedfellows indeed, she smiled to herself. All in all it was the best she could do, with no one's modesty being compromised and no temptation for hanky-panky. If only she'd known. How could she know? Lola was a woman, and Tangle didn't think like that.

Another problem was the lack of clothing. Most had been lost at *Crowned Crane Lodge* in the flood. Only Granville and Lola had been able to return to their rooms briefly. Granville had been ruthless. There must be no baggage on the trek. They were fighting for their lives, and everything else must be subordinate. Lola had accepted that, and in hindsight she'd been grateful. It'd been touch and go whether they'd make it and travelling light, with the exception of having to carry Chest, had made all the difference. But it had meant that the only clothes the refugees had at *Waters of Eostre* were the ones they'd worn on the journey. Those that were torn were mended, but their owners had to be closeted away naked or semi-naked while their garments were washed and dried. The solution was simple: they must share. Surprisingly, Rutt, Chest and Stanley were of roughly similar dimensions. Mo, Jake and Granville were very approximately interchangeable. Lola and Tangle could just about get by with sharing, in spite of Lola's slightly fuller figure, and even Teeny didn't look too absurd in Kirsten's things.

Drastic measures can have unexpected consequences. To Jake and Stanley, ill-fitting clothes belonging to someone else were either comical or embarrassing. To others, like Rutt and Mo, they could be sexy, if it was the women who were wearing them. As for Lola, her professional appreciation of Tangle's elegance was enhanced by wearing Tangle's dresses, tights and underwear, especially when they clung to her and gusseted so snugly against her skin. It was a new and legitimate way to experience Art, she told herself.

Kirsten was perfectly willing to take her newly charged phone up to the top of the hill two miles to the west, and she was happy to go alone. After all, she'd gone searching for reptiles and amphibians far and wide, and hadn't always had Joseph with her. Tangle was insistent, saying she must have an escort. It was as though the flood had been caused by some malevolent spirit which now lurked in the woods ready to pounce on fair maidens who were rash enough to venture forth basket in hand, metaphorically speaking. Kirsten gave up resisting, merely rolling her eyes when Tangle chose Jake to go with her.

At the top she turned this way and that, hoping for at least one bar on her phone.

Jake quickly grew impatient. 'Not getting anything?'

'I might if you stopped standing in the way.'

'Let me have a go.'

'No.' She stepped back from Jake and stumbled mildly on a tree root. '*Lort!*' She kept turning. 'There! Wait! I've got one, where's the list?'

Jake was slow in producing Tangle's list of contacts and emergency numbers.

'Forpulede rovhul!' All you had to do was be ready with that list.' She grabbed it from Jake. 'The signal's gone again. No, here it is.' She keyed in one of the numbers furiously. 'What? It's all in gibber-language. Swahili? Obooboan? I don't know. I can't understand anything. Here, read me out another number.' She keyed it in. 'Nothing. The signal has gone again. No, wait a minute! Give me that paper! No, nothing.'

'Come on, let me try.'

'No.'

'You've had long enough. You're getting tired.'

'I am not.'

Jake snatched at the phone while Kirsten tried to hold onto it. They tussled briefly. Kirsten managed to tighten her grip. Jake let go. Kirsten staggered backwards and the phone sailed through the air over her right shoulder, landing on a tree stump. The casing burst open. Both of them stared at the two pieces in disbelief which hadn't yet turned to horror. She advanced on him, mouth forward and arms rigid at her sides. *'Spasser! Knep dig selv! For fanden!'* Then she spun round and marched off down the hill without bothering to pick up the pieces.

Jake retrieved the phone, the part which still had the guts inside. He blew away the dirt then picked up the other. 'Obstinate little hussy,' he muttered to himself, sliding the casing back onto the phone. 'Still, the shock's probably broken it.' He looked for a signal. There wasn't one. He switched the phone off and on again. His eyes popped when he realised he was looking at two bars. He moved to his right. One bar. To his left, no bars. He moved back to where he'd got two bars. Still there. It was then that he realised the stupid girl had stormed off with Tangle's list of numbers. He didn't know any in Zuzubia. There was only one thing for it, he must summon help via Blighty. He dialled his sister in London.

'What's ya name and wot ya doin'?'

'Is that you, Toby?' It sounded like Jake's three-year-old nephew.

'It's Mr Splodges.'

'No you're not, you're Toby. Can I speak to Mummy, please?'

'I've been told not to speak to strangers.'

'I'm not a stranger, Toby, it's your Uncle Jake.'

'Mr Splodges says you're a liar.'

'That's not a very nice thing to say, Toby. Look, can I speak to your mother please?'

'I've got the trots. My Mummy says I must wash my hands after I've done poo-poos.'

'Yes, good, quite right, so you should.'

'And wipe my bottom.'

'Yes, I hope you do. Though strictly speaking it should be the other way round. Look, I really must speak to Mummy. This is an emergency.'

'Pop-pops. I've got the pop-pops.'

Jake let out a roar of exasperation. There was a long pause.

'Are you a naughty man? I'm coming to battle you. I think you're Darth Vader.' Toby gave a passable imitation of Jake's roar and Darth Vader at the same time. A long rambling account of the situation in Jedi-dom, or wherever it was, followed. Jake could hear a female voice in the background.

'Is that your Mummy I can hear?'

'She's stupid. She calls me the Caped Darth Vader.'

'No, well perhaps she does, but you're not, are you?'

'She's stupid. Don't you think she's stupid?'

'No, of course not. I mean yes, she's really stupid. Tell Mummy there's a man on the phone who thinks she's stupid.'

'You tell her.'

'How can I? I'm not there.'

'Where?'

'There. I mean here.'

The phone went dead. There was still a two-bar signal, so Jake concluded Toby must have cut him off. He tried to imagine the conversation. 'Who was that on the phone, darling?' 'Darth Vader.' 'I don't think so, dear. Did he leave a number?' There was the faintest of faint possibilities that Toby might in the end have admitted that it was Uncle Jake on the line. But so what? Kind of him to call, but she didn't really know where he was, somewhere in Africa, and it would be expensive to call back. Probably calling because it was Toby's birthday last week. He'd spoken to Toby now, so both would be happy.

Jake thought of calling again, but he didn't know how much credit Kirsten had on her phone, and he couldn't afford another long conversation with Toby. Who else? His friend Alex. Jake thought he knew his work number. Did it end 864 or 846? Or 684? Try 864.

'We *are* experiencing an *exceptional* number of calls at present. Your call *is* important to us. We *do* suggest you visit our website, which gives *all* the information about our products and services. Alternatively you can stay on the line. Your call *will* be answered shortly. You are currently... thirteenth in the queue. Your call will be answered in approximately thirty... six... minutes.'

Suddenly Jake remembered he knew the number of another friend, Matt Slater. This time he actually got through to a human being.

'Matt Slater, please.'

'Putting you through.' He could hear a ringing tone which seemed to go on for at least a minute.

'This is the voicemail of Matt Slater. Please leave a message and I'll return your call.'

Jake dialled again.

'I'm sorry about that, Sir. I'll try another line for you.' This time the ringing seemed to last even longer.

'All our personnel are attending a course on improving customer care. I'm afraid there's no one to take your call. Please try later.'

Jake dialled yet again and got the same operator for the third time.

'Oh dear, you don't seem to be having much luck today, do you Sir? I'll see if I can find Mr Slater myself.' Jake hung on for ages. 'Are you still there, Sir? I'm sorry about the delay. I've discovered Mr Slater is visiting our office in Birmingham. Would you like their number?' She gave it to him.

'Matt Slater. Hm. Let me see. Matt Slater. We don't seem to have anyone of that name working here. I'm afraid there's not much I...'

'He's visiting.' Jake just prevented himself from adding, 'You stupid idiot.'

'What department is he likely to be visiting?'

'He works in customer support.'

'We don't have a customer support department in Birmingham.' She sounded proud of the fact. 'We do have a marketing department. Shall I try them for you?'

'Yes please.'

'Marketing, Jenny speaking.'

'I'm trying to get hold of Matt Slater who's visiting, or so I've been told.'

'Not here.'

'Are you sure?'

'I think I would know. Would you like me to transfer you to sales?'

'Yes please.'

'Sales.'

'I've been trying to track down a Matt Slater from your London office, but no one seems to have heard of him.'

'Matt Slater. Hm. I don't know him personally, but I think I might know someone who's worked with him. Transferring you.'

'Bob!'

Jake asked the abrupt Bob if he knew where Matt Slater was.

'Transferring you.'

'This is the voicemail of Matt Slater. Please leave a message and I'll return your call.'

Jake roared at the phone. A large bird flew startled from the tree above. Some Obooboan children who'd been staring at him turned and fled.

It was getting late. In half an hour the light would start to fade. This being the tropics, it would get dark fast. He should get back. Try this first.

'You're through to Cyril,' said a voice with a distinctly, no indistinctly, un-Cyril-like accent. 'What serial number are you having, please?'

'My serial number?'

'Sir, it will be helping your enquiry if you will kindly be giving me your serial number.'

'I haven't got a serial number.'

'All our products are having serial numbers. Often it is to be looking on backside, isn't it?'

Jake hung up. One more call, the final one. 'Can I speak to Julia Simmons, please?'

'Are you deaf?'

'I beg your pardon?'

'I asked if you were deaf.'

'I heard you.'

'This line is only to assist deaf people.'

'Well, can't you put me through to the person I want to speak to?'

'I'm afraid I can only deal with your call if you are deaf.'

'I can't hear you!' Jake shouted and cut her off. He switched off the phone and started running back to *Waters of Eostre.*

Tangle had to enlist the support of Granville to keep the peace.

Kirsten was on fire. 'You used up all that time on

long distance calls? How could you? It is my money and I will make you pay for it.'

'So you don't think trying to get help is worth a few pounds? Anyhow, where were you? I was the one who managed to fix the thing and use it.'

'After you'd broken it!'

'I didn't. You were the one who threw it.'

'You were getting violent.'

'I most certainly was not. All I did was suggest that I have a go because you'd failed and were getting tired.'

'How gallant of you.'

Tangle tried to intervene. 'Look, it sounds like a misunderstanding.'

'Physically attacking me is not a misunderstanding.'

'I did not. I reached for the phone and you were so jumpy that you threw it over your shoulder.'

'That's nonsense! You snatched at it and when I hung on you started attacking me. Suddenly you let go and I was flung backwards, so I let go of the phone and it broke.'

'But it isn't broken! You couldn't even wait to see. I mended it for you and this is all the thanks I get. You flounced off without even leaving me with the list of numbers.'

'I think,' said Granville, 'that this sounds like one of those cases where mistakes have been made on both sides.' He held up his hand to silence objections. 'You have a phone that works and you have shown that you can make calls which get through. You should try again tomorrow.'

'Not with him!'

'I have heard enough.' Tangle was decisive. 'Too much, in fact. Kirsten, as it is your phone, you shall use it. I shall ask Mo to go with you tomorrow. Thank you, Jake. You have made a start, and for that we should all be grateful.'

CHAPTER NINETEEN

'How ya doin'? We've howdied but we ain't shook yet.' Kirsten peered at Rutt. Was he talking about the flood? 'You sure is purtee.'

'Excuse me?'

'Never seen such a looker in all my born days. Hope to be kicked to death by grasshoppers if I ain't tellin' the truth.' Rutt was making no allowance for the fact that Kirsten's first language wasn't Texan or even English. 'You's as cute as a possum. I sure would appreshate the time with y'all.'

'I think it is about ten o'clock.'

'When the sun's long gone and the moon's well ris, it's time for the wild thing.'

Kirsten made a bad mistake. She smiled. It was genuine amusement. She'd enjoyed *The Secluded Code*. Rutt had been good in it, but then he'd been acting out someone else's script.

Encouraged by her smile, Rutt posted his invitation. 'I sure would appreshate you doin' me the honour of rubbin' the bacon tonight. And if you're fixin' to saddle up, that's cool by me. Yonder cabin'll do just fine.'

For one fleeting moment, Kirsten enjoyed the attention of one of Hollywood's biggest stars, even if she couldn't understand a word he was saying. Her second smile conveyed the tiniest hint of flirtation. Then she walked on, dismissing him and his verbal froth from her mind.

Rutt had planned his visit carefully. He'd watched to see where Kirsten's room was. When he'd known everyone was at the main house, he'd examined ways of entering at night. The front door would be locked, and anyhow it would be impossible to get in that way without passing the old timer Granville Summers.

It didn't take him long to see how he could do it. There was a lean-to at the back which was used for storing boxes, crates, and cages. Although there was a door, Rutt knew it was locked at night. It was unlocked now with the key on the inside. He'd briefly shone a flashlight through the window the previous evening and there it had been, the key in the lock. All he had to do was shut the window now in such a way that it looked tightly closed, open it when he got there, reach down, turn the key and let himself in through the door. He could then climb the stairs to Kirsten's room without passing Granville, who slept downstairs at the front. As she'd be expecting him, she would open her bedroom door and he would slip in.

Kirsten thought she heard creaking sounds coming from downstairs. She sat up in bed. It was probably Granville moving about, but it seemed as though the noises were coming from her specimen room immediately below. What would he be doing in there? There was a particularly loud clatter which made her swing her feet out of bed. She was about to go downstairs and investigate when she heard footsteps on the stairs. Someone was coming up, and they were moving very slowly. It was that which convinced her that Granville, if it was Granville, was up to no good. She slid from her bed and moved to the corner nearest the door. Fortunately the moon was shining fully into the room, so she could see everything clearly. Her heart was beating fast. She struggled to control her breathing. Still the footsteps came on. She could sense that Granville was standing just the other side of the door. She looked round for a weapon but could see none. There were five quiet taps on the door, two of them slow and the other three in rapid succession. She suddenly remembered something. She tiptoed lightly across the room and reached into her wardrobe. She'd put a net for catching specimens in there a week ago, meaning to repair its broken handle sometime. She glided silently back to the door.

'Who is it?'

'Me.' Apart from the fact it was a male voice, that hadn't told her anything.

'What do you want?'

'I'm here.' That didn't sound like Granville.

The door opened and the man, obviously of large stature, came in quickly.

Rutt was completely taken by surprise. The moon temporarily dazzled him, something hit him on the nose and his upper arms seemed to be pinned to his sides. He could sense what felt like a net over his face. He was being shoved backwards out of the room. He fell back into nothing but air and then bounced twice on the upper stairs. He managed to twist so that his hand grabbed a rail to arrest his fall, but momentum and the weight of his body caused him to swing round and bang his head painfully on a wall. With his other hand he pulled the net up over his head and tumbled down the remaining stairs. Panting, he staggered into the storeroom just as Granville appeared from the front of the house. Hearing voices behind him, Rutt crawled his way across the clutter of packing cases and boxes towards the outer door, stumbling and scrambling, finally flinging himself out into the moonlight.

Kirsten's coolness under pressure had dissolved. She sat shaking and gulping on her bed while Granville tried to comfort her. She'd been totally silent during the tussle with Rutt, not even swearing at him in Danish while she'd driven him from the room. Even now there were more snivels than words. Would she like him to get Tangle? No. Would she like a drink? Yes please. Tea, coffee or something stronger? Cocoa. Do you know where I might find it? Cupboard to the right of the sink. It was nearly half an hour before Granville felt he could ask whether she was all right now, hinting that he might leave. She nodded assent.

Bufo Sayeri hadn't liked it one little bit when his cage had started quaking and what seemed like a terrifying predator had come crashing into his domain. It had passed quite quickly, but by that time he'd been tipped on his side. His whole world seemed to have been knocked through ninety degrees. He soon recovered and crawled forward. And forward. And forward some more. That pen, or at least part of it, seemed to have disappeared. He walked onwards towards the light, his slow pace quickening. The nearer he got to it, the more he could feel the lure of the forest and a greater urge which drew him on even faster. He passed through the door and out into the moonlight. A terrible commotion came hurtling from behind, and what seemed like a giant tree casting a huge shadow thundered onto the earth beside him and was gone. He'd frozen in terror, but now he looked around. He smelt the air. It seemed that paradise lay to the left. He started walking again.

At Kirsten's insistence, Rutt had been excluded from the search party to find the toad. He'd dropped in the disfavour rankings even lower than Jake, who was allowed to participate, if only as a further snub to Rutt. She'd allocated them each a sector of the gardens and forest, while she moved between them giving advice. Even Teeny was taking part. Kirsten had insisted that they study her many photos of *Bufo Sayeri* from all angles, even those who thought they were familiar with him. She arranged for each person to have a stick, 'to part the vegetation carefully, not to beat about the bush.' Kirsten's idiomatic English wasn't perfect.

'Not like that, Stanley,' Jake had called across to him. 'You'll pulverise a constipated toad into a pile of diarrhoea. Gently! Look, like this, see?'

After an hour had passed, Kirsten blew a whistle and they all reassembled. Had anybody seen anything? They hadn't.

The only one to report anything of interest was Teeny. 'There's a fallen tree over there. I looked underneath. I do hope your toad hasn't been squashed, Kirsten.' They all went to look, peering under the trunk from all angles. They could see nothing.

'Well, if it is under there it'll be a case of hole in the toad.'

'We could do without that, Jake,' said Mo. 'This is serious business. How would you feel if you were Kirsten?'

'The same as I always do when Jake's around.' Kirsten sounded more depressed than angry. They searched for another hour, each widening their sector according to Kirsten's instructions. This time they reconvened in the big room of the main house for coffee.

'Found it yet?' boomed Chest. 'You will. The thing can't have crawled far. It can't because it can't. Doesn't move fast enough.'

'There's something in that,' said Granville.

'I saw a toad, but it was the wrong sort.'

'What do you mean, Stanley?' Mo wasn't the only one staring at him.

'It was too big. I know what Kirsten's toad looks like. I've seen it lots of times. This one was much bigger and it didn't look the same.'

'Come on,' Kirsten called over her shoulder as she sprinted across the room and out towards Stanley's sector. Mo and Jake bundled Stanley out the door after her.

Long before the others could catch up, Kirsten saw the toad, her toad, sitting on a rock. Or so she thought. She stood there as the others rushed up to her, almost knocking her over. Her eyes were flaring.

'That's...' Stanley stopped. 'That's not the one I saw. Isn't that one yours, Kirsten'? I saw a much bigger one.'

'I can't believe it,' she breathed.

'Neither can he,' said Jake.

'It's a female and they're mating.'

'He's enjoying the biggest belly ride in Africa. Makes you realise what you were missing last night, Kirsten.'

'Go to your room!' Tangle was not a violent person, but Jake started backing away as she advanced on him. 'I mean it. Now! At once!'

'Are you saying,' said Mo slowly, 'that this female here is the same species as... the one on top of it... and that she too is – was - extinct?'

They'd never seen Kirsten so radiant as she turned to look up at him. 'That is what I am saying. But the female has never been recorded before.'

They all queued up to hug her, all except Jake, who'd obediently returned to his room.

'Sayer was right. They don't mate in water. No tadpoles. That's what Chuck Larter said.' Kirsten was talking to herself, because no one else knew what she was on about.

Rutt's double transgression and the search for the toad had set them back several hours. Kirsten could no longer afford the time to walk to the top of the hill with her phone, so Mo took Jake instead.

'You're not touching it. Kirsten would go ape. But since you do know how to use it when you're not breaking it...'

'And mending it.'

'You might as well come along and tell me what you did to make it work.'

Tangle assigned Granville and Stanley to walk round the rock and report on progress with the floods. She herself would drive in the van with Lola and see how far they got. The disgraced Rutt would stay with Chest and Teeny so that Chest, in his own words, 'would talk some sense into that young man.'

Mo failed to make a single call. Soon after he switched on the phone he received a message, 'Your credit has expired. Top up now and you can make 20 free calls over the next three days. Terms & conditions apply.'

'Oh boy, she's going to love that, Jake. I think you've just regained your place at the bottom of the pack. In view of what Rutt's tried to do to her over the past twenty-four hours, that's quite an achievement.'

Tangle drove along the road which snaked from the rock down towards the plain. She was conscious that Lola had slewed round in her seat and was staring at her. A wise woman speaks because she has something to say. A foolish woman speaks because she has to say something. What that pithy saying ignores is that a woman may be forced to speak because she is embarrassed, whether foolish or not. Tangle started clucking like a hen caught canoodling with a rabbit in the headlights.

'Jake. It was Jake who drove down here yesterday. Stanley was with him.' She glanced at Lola who, to her dismay, was smiling fully at her. 'They didn't get far. I expect we may get further today. Am I going too fast?'

'No.'

'Or too slowly perhaps?'

'You're doing it perfectly. You do.'

'What do you mean?'

'Everything you do, you do perfectly. Ever since I arrived here, I've been observing you.'

'You've...'

'Mind out!'

'Sorry.' Tangle had swerved violently to avoid a rock which had fallen out of the bank.

'See? You reacted so coolly. Your movements are graceful and economic. You didn't panic.'

I did, thought Tangle, and I'm panicking now.

'I'm an appreciator of Art. Observation is my profession.' That statement would have alarmed Tangle less if Lola hadn't still been staring at her.

They reached the bottom of the hill. Tangle flung up a despairing hand. 'Damn! I really thought we might get further. Look.' They both stared at the road ahead, which vanished into several feet of water. 'This is as far as Jake got yesterday. Exactly the same place.'

'Why don't we get out and take a look? It's beautiful and I'd like to linger.'

'No, we must be getting back.' Tangle's voice had risen to a flustered squeak. 'There's lots to do.' She swung the van round and accelerated hard up the hill, breathing heavily.

Granville's report gave a better picture. 'The floodwaters have retreated quite a lot. The river's still in spate, but beyond it we could see large areas of grass and scrub where there was nothing but water before. It's better to the east than it is to the south.'

'It's to the south where the road is. I've just been there with Lola. It's under several feet of water for as far as we could see.'

They all agreed that they were still marooned.

CHAPTER TWENTY

They were assembling for dinner. In spite of slotting in an extra table, it was still a tight squeeze. Chest, wedged between Rutt and Teeny, was in some pain. With ten people in a confined space, it was important that they should all get along together.

Lola, the last to arrive, sashayed in wearing a lemon-yellow dress. It had fitted the narrow figure of Tangle perfectly, but on Lola it hugged and clung provocatively.

Jake fluttered his eyebrows. 'Looks like you've slipped on a banana skin.'

Lola responded with an impish smile and a flick of a hip.

Jake wasn't the only one with his eyes on her.

'Ay-yay-yay, bei mir bist du shayn.'

Lola paused and stared at Mo with a look which conveyed first disbelief, then amusement and finally new possibilities. He'd spoken Yiddish. *'A sheynem dank. Vee geyts? Nu, fershtay?'*

'Not another one,' Jake tutted. 'These Welsh get everywhere.'

They were nearing the end of the meal when the ruction started, innocently at first.

'If no help arrives tomorrow,' said Mo, 'how about we get back to the gardens? All those vegetables and fruit won't find their way to our table if we don't take care of them. If you agree Tangle, we'll await your orders in the morning?'

'Can I help, if someone can tell me what to do?'

Tangle was delighted. 'That's very kind of you, Lola. Mo, Stanley, and Jake, they're all experts now, they'll show you. We practise strictly organic permaculture here. We work with Nature, following her biorhythms, making sure that everything we take from her is sustainable. We only use tools which are sympathetic to the sensibilities of the soil. We are the servants of the Earth, not her mistress.'

'Spare me this sustainability moonshine.' The *Waters of Eostre* natives, even Stanley, slewed round to stare at Chest. 'What we need is a good steak, eh Rutt?'

'Sure do, and we ain't pernickety about what it's been fed on, nor what's been done to fetch it to the table.'

Chest continued, 'Heavy machinery? Fine, bigger the better. Trees in the way, cut 'em down! The Big Country. We ain't ashamed of that where we come from.'

'We'll assume you mean that in jest,' said Mo coldly. 'Let's move on.'

'No, I ain't kiddin'. All this talk about climate

change and global warming and telling everyone to return to the land with flint tools in their hands, it's all a load of hogwash if you ask me.'

'I find that rather insulting,' said Jake. 'You're Tangle's guest. She took you in as a charitable act and all you can do is scoff at her way of life.'

'Did I? Well I'm sorry, Tangle, I don't mean to give no offence. It's just the preachiness of it all that browns me off. It's kinda like you're ramming this stuff down our throats. In the US we're a free society, live and let live. That means rights for all, the freedom to do things how I want, yes and that includes driving around in the biggest SUV you've seen in your darned life and putting a row of fifteen combines to work in one field. It means the freedom to buy up new land and erect my own fence and pay my own guards to keep it the way I want. If some meddlin' killjoy out of Washington feels minded to go pokin' around a man's real estate, don't tell me I don't have the right to put some buckshot in his ass. We've grown great by kicking ass. No one tells me where to walk so that I don't tread on a bacteria.' Chest neither knew nor cared about the nitpicketiness of grammar, but he could do sarcasm. 'Stop, no I mean it, stop! You're traumatising the stones. All that garbage has no part in our lives. That right, Rutt? You're fixin' to run for Congress. Ain't that what you stand for?'

'Sure is, Chest. That's the Tea Party message.'

'Messages are for the Western Union,' said Granville so quietly that no one heard him.

Jake put the boot in. 'You should know, Rutt.

Your qualifications are impeccable. Acting is the most minor of gifts. After all, Shirley Temple could do it at the age of four.'

Chest, who should have been defending Rutt against Jake, couldn't help himself. 'Katherine Hepburn! Kate Hepburn said that!'

Jake was at them again. 'Of course a semi-automatic weapon is essential to you Americans so you can kill twenty moose a minute, once you've run out of Minority Americans.'

That did rile Rutt. 'You're as full of wind as a corn-eating horse. You think the sun comes up just to hear you crow.'

Jake dissolved into laughter. He tried to imitate Rutt's Texan drawl but could hardly get his words out. 'Is that a rooster blasting off through his rear end while crowing, or a cock-a-doodling horse?'

Chest rode to Rutt's rescue. 'Hey son, were you bullied at school?'

'I was,' said Stanley. 'I was called Prick the Sausage.'

'You told us,' said Mo, glad for the conversation to be diverted. 'They were very cruel to you, Stanley, especially as you were partially deaf.'

'I was, but I'm better now. When I was six I was picking at my ear wax with a pin. I sneezed.'

Chest struggled to his feet and thrust an angry finger at Jake. 'What you need, young man, is to grow up.'

'Sit down you old fool. You're like a running sore with a bare head.'

'Now you look here.'

'You're a fossil. The only part of you functioning is the jawbone of an ass.'

'I've had enough of this.' Kirsten stood up and left the room.

Teeny now intervened. 'What we need is to return to good honest Christian values.'

'That's right, my Princess, you tell 'em. Let your light shine on these poor people in their darkness and let them know what we believe in.'

Jake put his head in his hands. 'Oh God!'

Teeny ploughed on. 'Whenever I feel my Faith becoming dim, I think of my dead grandmother. She had Faith which never wavered, so I call her up.'

'That's handy!'

'And I see her standing before me with her unwavering Faith, and I know that I must believe for her sake.'

'Your belief,' Lola sneered, 'is to please someone... who's dead?' And so another generation becomes doomed to credulity and unreality.'

Teeny, still smarting from Lola's attack yesterday on her psychoanalyst encouraging her to get rid of her teenage children, retaliated, 'As someone who hasn't yet seen the Light, you may be forgiven for your primitive views.'

This dig at Lola's newly revealed Jewishness offended her racial integrity but not her religion. 'You don't know what my beliefs are. You're so bigoted that you think yours is the One True Faith. Why do you think God allows so many different versions of himself? Has he instructed all those varieties of believers to contradict each other on his behalf? If so, he's the ultimate masochist, always attacking himself. As for you, all you can do is hide behind your dead grandmother. Have you actually heard her speak since she died?'

'Are you calling my wife a liar?'

'Only until I can think of something worse to call her.'

'Ladies, ladies, your hormones are showing.' Jake was enjoying this. 'In my country we have what's called the Established Church. It means that politics, religion, and royalty are all hopelessly muddled up together. That's why we sing 'God Save the Queen'. Unfortunately Charles and Camilla really do exist.'

'So what do you believe in,' Chest spat at him, 'other than yourself?'

'Oh my religion's simple. I believe we're all part of a big compost heap. The universe is only one tiny bit of it.'

'What makes you think that?'

Jake opened the palms of his hands. 'Precisely. My theory's as fanciful as yours.'

In all his fury, Chest had forgotten about Rutt, who any moment might begin spouting all that bull he'd picked up from Hoki Kokum or whatever that faker called himself. But Rutt wasn't there; he'd left the room some time ago. Chest hadn't noticed, but Granville had. The whole conversation had been ridiculous and Granville wanted no part of it. To him religion was simple. In the balance of probability, a supreme being may have created the universe. No one knew, no one could tell, and any further invented detail was baseless. If people wanted to believe that it was meritorious to puff incense about or not eat pork, that was up to them. There was no point arguing about it. When he'd noticed Rutt leave the room not long after Kirsten, Granville had slipped out after him. He'd considered it his duty to return to the house to protect her from any more hanky-panky from that Hollywood film star.

They were so worked up now that no one noticed a tear wandering slowly down Tangle's cheek.

Red in the face and clearly in pain, Chest stood up for a second time. 'You intellectual smart-asses can wank away - I'm sorry, Angel, but these creeps have got my dander up - can go on as much as they like with their liberal filth, but the majority of us stick to the path the Good Lord has laid down for us. I'm a simple guy who gets his instructions from God.'

'That saves you taking responsibility for your actions.'

Chest closed his eyes to shut out Jake, took a deep breath and continued. 'In my humble opinion...'

'Why don't you sit down with your humble opinion? What you lack is blather control.'

'Come on, Sweetheart, I've heard more ordure tonight than in all of my lifetime.' Chest started ushering Teeny from the room. She was sobbing. 'I hope you're enjoying what you've done to her.'

No one spoke for a long time after, not even Jake. One by one they got up and silently left the room.

In her bedroom, Tangle was distraught. She'd just heard that her cook had walked out, but that was the least of her worries. All this negative energy, all this outward spiralling, all this bickering, it was the fault of the water, which was behaving as badly as the men. Lola could see Tangle's distress, how she paused as she was about to do up the bow of her nightie, how she stood up and walked to the window, staring as though the curtains didn't exist.

'It must be hard for you.'

Tangle didn't turn towards her immediately. When she did so, Lola patted her bed indicating that Tangle should sit down beside her. 'Tell me.'

'It used to be so calm here. The levitational quality of the groundwater derived from the aqueous fluids within the earth. Their lymphatic flow was so pure. It was soft and feminine, undefiled and untrammelled. The things we grew last year! You could feel the fertility rising like dew through the soil. In the mornings you could breathe the fecundity, you could feel the invisible currents channelling through the air. The memory of procreation rose imprinted within the feminine potential, creating a duality which recognised and responded to the call for renewal.'

Since this was a bucolic form of the way Lola talked herself, she was most impressed. She didn't understand precisely what Tangle meant, but Great Art did not need to be - indeed should not be - precise. 'What a paradise it must have been,' she purred. 'You're so clever. Tell me more about the feminine potential.'

'The water develops a maternal, ovigenous potential that is generative. It is modest, it is virginal, but it is responsive to kindness, to love and to gentleness. It is at the same time chaste and desirous of coupling. Can you understand that?'

Lola couldn't, but she sure was sympathetic to the sensuousness of Tangle and her words. Dare I? I do. 'So the moistness, the wetness of the feminine potential is a response to the caress of a sensitive and loving hand?' Tangle, only a few inches away from her on the bed, turned towards her. Was this the moment?

'But then it all changed!' Tangle half-shrieked. 'Hot, aggressive floodwater came spiralling down the river. New water evolved in the atmosphere, giving the earth a masculine potential. The flow became fiery and vindictive. Anger infiltrated the soil, saturating it. And with it came the men.'

Ah, the men, thought Lola. Is Tangle anti-men? Is she, can she be? She put a hand on Tangle's shoulder, stroking it gently.

'Oh, I don't know.' Tangle leapt to her feet. 'Perhaps I'm being unfair. Mo's a good man,' she turned to Lola passionately, 'a good man. Stanley, well, he's innocent, wouldn't hurt a fly, and Jake, he gets on people's nerves but he's a good worker, loves it and I believe loves the way we do things here. These new men, how can they be expected to understand when they're so rich and so new, look you? They came with the flood. Was it their fault? I don't know.'

She'd moved across to her bed and got in. 'Anyhow, talking about it now won't solve the problem, will it? The flood will go down, it must. The world will turn as it always has and always will. Tomorrow will be another day. Thank you for listening to me. Goodnight.'

CHAPTER TWENTY-ONE

After Kwame, gazing through tear-dimmed eyes, had lost sight of his Lady, seeing her first become a hippo and then an elephant, it had taken him several hours to get back to *Crowned Crane Lodge*. When he got there, he found it deserted. Still grieving for his lost Love, he surveyed the wreckage of the hotel; but when he peered into what remained of the dining room, he broke down and could look no more.

He spent a miserable night in strange luxury sleeping in one of the few guests' beds which hadn't been destroyed. He managed to forage some food next day and drank the water which Granville Summers had deemed unsafe. His family lived forty miles to the south, and he knew that for the time being it would be impossible to reach them. A vague idea swam into his head. Some big *bwanas* would come to *Crowned Crane Lodge* sooner or later. There would be work to be done salvaging, rebuilding and eventually re-staffing the hotel. No one else was here, so he would be in prime position to be re-employed. His best - indeed his only - option was to stay put.

The following afternoon, one of the cleaners appeared. He told Kwame how he'd seen a party of white men and women leave the hotel several hours after the flood had struck. They'd headed west, returned, then headed north. No, the large lady was not among them. The cleaner, who knew the area much better than Kwame, didn't know where they were going. The only habitation within twenty miles was high on a cliff to the west. Yes, it was on, or rather above, the river. No, he hadn't been there, but he'd heard that several Europeans lived there. Why had the party headed north? He didn't know. Perhaps it was because of the flood.

In a flash of hope or rather faith, Kwame speculated. What if Madam had managed to survive? What if the river had taken her far downstream, way beyond where he'd had to turn back? He seemed to recall seeing what looked like a rock a few miles beyond the elephant. What if Madam had been swept there, had managed to climb ashore and taken refuge?

The more he dithered that afternoon, the more desire carried him to one conclusion. Madam could be there, so he had to go there. He would start out early the next morning.

Although the floods had subsided greatly since Granville, Lola, Rutt, Chest and Teeny had made the journey to *Waters of Eostre,* Kwame's walk was still slow, dangerous, and uncomfortable. But he made it in one day, arriving in the late afternoon. His walk ended with one piece of good fortune. It wasn't Jake or Stanley who answered the door but Tangle herself.

'Is the Lady here?'

Those who knew Tangle Breeze admired her for many reasons, one of which was that she was superb at dealing with Zuzubians, from bigwig officials to the humblest of servants. She was patient, fair, considerate, and respectful, never rushing them, unlike many Europeans.

'We have several ladies here. I am one of them.'

Kwame looked at the thin figure before him and shuddered. Even by the standards of most European women, this *muzungu* was like a talking skeleton. 'I want to see your ladies.'

'Well, other than me, there's, let me see, one, two, three others. You do mean a white woman, I take it?'

'Yes, white woman.'

Tangle thought. She didn't know where Lola, Teeny and Kirsten were right now, but in a couple of hours they would be assembling for dinner. What dinner? Tangle, who didn't regard herself as much of a cook, would have to prepare it herself.

'You are looking for a lady who you think might be here?'

'She sit in river, Madam.'

Tangle knew that laughing at a Zuzubian was not the same as laughing at a European. Laughter, especially directed at a stranger, conveyed discomfort and embarrassment. So she didn't laugh.

'Can I ask your name, please?'

'It is Kwame, Madam.'

'Well, Kwame, before we go any further, I need to know a bit about you. Where have you come from?'

'I come from *Crowned Crane Lodge*, Madam.'

That makes things easier, thought Tangle. Even her generosity of spirit baulked at letting a strange African into *Waters of Eostre*. But his credentials could soon be verified by any of the refugees from *Crowned Crane Lodge*. Even so, if Kwame was looking for Lola or Teeny (he would hardly be looking for Kirsten), Tangle needed to know why. She was diverted by a flash of inspiration.

'Can you cook, Kwame?'

'Madam?'

'Can you cook? Can you prepare food and cook it for us to eat?'

'I have been in the kitchen at *Crowned Crane Lodge*.' That was an impressive answer. It wasn't a lie; Kwame had been in the kitchen many times, in and out, collecting and delivering food to the dining room.

Tangle became decisive. 'Right, here's what we'll do. You can cook our meal tonight. I'll pay you fifteen *dinkwas* and you can sleep on the veranda. When the guests appear, I'll let you see them, then perhaps you will find your lady. If you cook well tonight, I'll take you on for one week's trial. If that works out, I will take you on permanently. Is that fair?'

'Yes, Madam.'

'There's ten of us. Do you think you could manage that?'

'Yes, Madam.'

'Good, then I'll show you the kitchen and the storeroom. I've got a couple of ideas for the meal tonight and you can choose one of them. Come with me.'

Tangle showed Kwame the kitchen. He lifted the lids of the range, just to look impressive, and peered into a big white box which appeared to be wired into the wall. He knew what taps were, so he turned them on and off again, nodding wisely as each one spouted water. He couldn't see any food, apart from a bowl of fruit. Most *muzungu* ate meat - they expected it every day - or fish, but he couldn't see either. Hopefully they were in one of those cupboards.

The Lady solved his dilemma for him. 'The stores are up the track by that house you can see in the trees. There's a cart to wheel them down in. We'll go there now.'

They left the kitchen and turned towards the buildings where Kirsten and now Granville lived. They'd only gone about twenty metres when a panting Jake burst round the corner of the main house. 'Electrics gone, the whole caboodle. I've tried the fuses. Nothing.'

Tangle had been dreading this. It had been a miracle that they'd only lost communications when the flood had first struck, not electricity. She recovered her composure quickly. 'The generator. We had a new one delivered three months ago, remember? It's in the lean-to next to my office. All ready to use, see? Powerful.' Jake delighted in the Welshness of the way she said that. 'I bought it because they told me it could keep the whole place going if we lost electricity.'

Jake was up for it. 'Right, let's get the old girl cranked up. Who knows how?'

Tangle looked thoughtful. 'Well, let me see now, it's Joseph.' Her face fell.

'And?'

'And, well, no one, just Joseph. I made sure he tested it. It worked perfectly.'

'You know where Joseph is, don't you?'

'I do,' said Tangle obstinately, trying to avoid sounding guilty.

'On leave, a long way away. The other side of a hundred miles of floodwater.'

'All right, Jake,' she snapped. 'Sometimes I think you revel in misfortune.' She brightened. 'There's an instruction booklet. I'm sure we'll get it working between us. Where's Mo? Oh yes, I remember, he's taken the van to get firewood with Stanley and Rutt.'

'And won't be back until dark,' Jake added.

'We'll have to get it going ourselves, won't we?' Tangle sounded defiant. 'Come on, what are you waiting for?' Jake caught the faintest of smiles.

Kwame wondered what they were talking about. At times they'd seemed to be arguing, but in the end it appeared they'd made up because they walked off together back to the house. Was he meant to follow? They hadn't asked him to. The Lady, the real Lady, his Madam, flooded into his mind. He tingled at the thought that she might be close by. This was his opportunity to look for her. He might as well start searching in that house up the hill. That way he could inspect the stores at the same time and choose something to cook for their suppers.

Tangle and Jake stared at the generator. 'I thought you didn't like machines, Tangle?'

'I don't. But needs must, as they say. And before you start asking, Jake, yes we do have enough fuel; there it is in that tank outside.'

Jake beamed at her. 'You are wonderful, you know that?' He meant it.

Tangle tilted a shoulder to hide her embarrassment and started twiddling her hair. 'Come on, we haven't got all day. I'll sing out the instructions. You do whatever they say.'

'I'd love to hear you sing. Could you start with *Hen Wlad Fy Nhadau*? All Welsh people know that. I find it very moving.'

This time Tangle actually laughed. 'Right. *Before operating this product, please read ALL the safety instructions.* ALL is in capitals, so I suppose we'd better. Here goes. *Use in a suitable manner only.* What's that supposed to mean? Absolutely nothing. *This product is only suitable for the purposes intended.*'

'It means do not use it as a toilet or for the detonation of nuclear devices.'

'Amongst a million other things. I'll read on. *This product is a tripping hazard. Please site it where no injury may take place to any persons in the vicinity.* Are we wasting our time here?'

'Not at all. These things are very important, matters of life and death. This product may contain nuts. As well as bolts. For your safety when using this equipment, breathe with care. Breathing can be dangerous. Use only the manufacturer's recommended breathing apparatus and breathe evenly at a rate of between twenty-four and twenty-nine intakes a minute.'

'Oh shut up, Jake! This is confusing enough without you dreaming up further silliness. Come on. *Heating hazard. Your generator's exhaust may be very hot.* Not at this rate. *Always place your generator in a safe place on solid, level ground away from buildings.* Well, this is solid and level.'

'But hardly away from buildings. It's in one. I think you're only meant to use it outside.'

'Am I?'

'I think it produces carbon monoxide.'

'I thought it was meant to produce electricity.'

'Tangle, I do believe you're being flippant.'

'Well, really! *Electricity can kill.* You don't say? *Do not touch your generator if you have wet hands.* How about tongues?

'Is that an invitation? You're making me blush, Tangle.'

'*Do not operate in wet conditions.* Has to be outside, not in wet conditions, in central Africa in the rainy season.'

'We could try it here briefly, then when the others come back we could move it outside and put some kind of awning over it.'

'All right, Jake, one more try. Bother! Look what it says here. *These instructions cover models TD165, TD168, RD172, RZ459 and RZ471.* We still haven't found out which model ours is.'

'It's on the label here. It's an RZ459.'

'Yes, but how do we know which instructions apply to the RZ whatever you just said? Oh, here it is. *For full instructions relating to your particular model, see outer packaging.*'

'Which you've thrown away?'

'No I haven't. Do you think I'm daft or what?'

'I think you're wonderful, Tangle.'

'Yes, well, here it is. What does it say? *For instructions on how to start your generator, visit our website on www...* How can we do that? We've got no communications!'

'And no electricity. It's starting to get dark, Tangle.'

'I can see it is. Do you know what I think we should do? There's a stock of candles locked away in my office. I think we should put those out and leave this flipping thing until morning, or at least until after dinner when the others are back. Mo will know what to do. I bet he can work it, instructions or no instructions.' Tangle had gone dreamy.

Jake snorted. Much as he liked Mo, he was jealous of Tangle's fawning over him.

'Come on, Jake, let's find the candles and spread them around.'

Walking into the dining room, Tangle was surprised to see Kwame. She'd completely forgotten about him and that he wouldn't be able to cook without electricity. 'I'm sorry to have neglected you, Kwame, I've been occupied. I know you won't be able to serve a cooked meal. Come on, we'll go to the stores and see what we can eat cold.'

'It is all right, Madam. I have under control. I have lighted a fire with some wood and you will like my hot food. I have found food in the store myself. You will like it.'

This display of initiative and confidence so impressed Tangle that she decided to leave him to it. Some of the others were starting to appear and she needed to help Jake spread the candles out.

Everyone could sense that the tensions were different tonight. Those from *Crowned Crane Lodge* who'd made their pile and those from *Waters of Eostre* who were up to their necks in theirs had grown used to each other's eccentricities. In any case, they were exhausted from trying to mock their differences. An uneasy truce pervaded the dining room, with a growing realisation that this would almost certainly be the last night when they would all be intimately together. The floodwaters were subsiding, but somehow the image seemed to be the reverse, of floodgates about to be thrown open. They were apprehensive of rescue, whatever that might mean. This was, after all, a remote part of darkest Africa, and they were under a dictatorship.

'I'll get that generator going when we've finished eating,' said Mo. 'Let's concentrate now on tomorrow. We just don't know who's going to arrive first. When Haiti had its big earthquake, all the best transport including helicopters was appropriated by journalists, even ahead of relief workers.'

That was right up Jake's street. 'It's rarely those who need it most who get the attention. Once the lawyers get going, it's the outsiders who've been traumatised by witnessing horrors that get the compensation, not those who've suffered them. Take Bhopal.'

'Don't let's,' said Lola. Like many round the table, she couldn't face another night of bitchiness towards the Americans.

Jake heeded her only to the extent of dropping the subject of Bhopal. 'There was a case last year in America. A customer found the Chef's severed fingertip in his yoghurt and refused to give it back. The staff begged him to hand it over so it could be rushed to hospital to be sewn back on again, but the customer refused, insisting he keep it as evidence for his lawsuit.'

Several round the table felt like telling Jake to pipe down, but knew that this would only encourage him. He was met by an icy silence which was much more effective.

Kwame stood motionless in the doorway, his eyes passing rapidly over the faces. No one had noticed him yet. He recognised Teeny, Lola and Tangle, which left only one other lady. He stared at Kirsten, unable to take in that his mission had failed. Madam was not here. She had gone, gone forever, taken by the river.

Suddenly Teeny noticed him. 'Look!' she squeaked, pointing rudely. 'From the hotel, that waiter. Odile! Odile's…'

Tangle looked in horror as Kwame, hearing that name, shuddered with grief. He turned away in an attempt to stifle a wail. Tangle followed him through to the kitchen where he stood with his hands on the sink looking as though he was about to vomit. She knew better than to touch him. Very tenderly she leaned across and quietly comforted him. 'I understand. Your lady is not here. It is all right to be sad. I will look after you. Show me where the food is and I will serve it.'

Kwame looked up, staring deep into the compassion of this lady. He drew strength from her simple humility. He had never received this sort of kindness from a *muzungu* before, let alone a stick. 'I will put the food onto the plates, Madam, you will take it to the peoples.' He broke down again, not thinking of Odile but of the goodness of this lady. All their next actions took place to the snuffling coming from Kwame. He led Tangle outside to where he'd lit a neat fire between a small quadrangle of stones. The largest pot from the kitchen was perched on a metal mesh. He lifted the lid. 'Stew.'

Tangle pretended to smell the aroma. Being a vegan, she knew she would gag if she inhaled it. But it looked good for those who needed such things, dark and rich and the right consistency. He'd boiled some yams for the carbohydrate, and although there didn't seem to be any green vegetables, this was a good first performance. Tangle sighed. She was resigned to cobbling some leaves for herself to go with the yams. She brought the plates and a large tray and asked Kwame to dish up nine portions of stew with yams. Holding her breath, she took the food to the dining room, where the candlelight flickered on the beams. She served it to the eager diners. She was pleasantly surprised to find that no one was bickering.

Mo seemed to be getting them to focus on their

priorities for tomorrow. 'Tangle, we've been trying to agree what's most important when help does start to arrive. Three things seem to stand out: medical treatment for Chest, replenishment of food stocks, and whatever gets thrown at us because of the toad.'

'Don't worry about me,' thundered Chest. 'I'm as sound as a dollar.'

'Almost true, but not quite.' Granville smiled at him in a serious way. 'You've made a remarkable recovery. When we arrived here, I was fairly sure that infection would set in. It hasn't, I'm pleased to say, but your leg still needs to be reset. It's an operation, and that means a hospital, but at least you're well past the stage of trauma.'

'The moment the door's unbolted, I'm gonna cut ass like shit out of a goose.'

'A dainty image, Rutt, if rather a mixed metaphor.' Rutt hadn't a clue what Jake was on about, so it was easy to ignore him. 'You sound a tad ungrateful.'

'You'll all want to get onto your travel and insurance companies and I expect you have agents,' said Mo soothingly, addressing the refugees.

'I'd like to stay for a while and help.' Several of them swung round to face Lola. 'I admire what you're doing here, and if I can be of use to help you get back to normality then I will.'

Tangle half-choked. She didn't think she could take much more emotion in one day. 'Thank you,' she said huskily.

'This stew's terrific, Tangle. I thought you said you'd lost your cook.'

'I had, Mo, but then Kwame arrived from

Crowned Crane Lodge, so I offered him the job. I'm glad you like it.'

Mo continued, 'Where were we? Chest needs to get to hospital. Teeny, you'll want to go with him. Rutt, you can't wait to get away. Lola, you're staying. Granville?'

'I'll go with Chest until it's clear whether it's best to have that operation in Kumbala or the States. If it's Kumbala, I'll stay with him until I'm sure they know what they're doing.'

'Granville, you're a real butt-kicker. Haven't seen an act of generosity like it since Bogey gave up that seat on the plane in *Casablanca*.'

Lola was less generous. 'What about your baby, Teeny? Won't you need to get back to Benjamin?'

'Oh don't worry about him. I'm sure he'll be fine. He probably won't have cleared customs yet.'

Mo returned to his agenda. 'Next item, food.'

'We're not exactly starving,' said Tangle. We'll need to replenish the stores as soon as we can, and get our own produce to market again. Until we get that generator working, we can't store any perishables, but we've run them down in any case. This must be the last of the meat you're eating now.'

'That does it. I fer sher ain't perching my ass here no longer. This stoo's yummy, but it ain't no t-bone.'

Mo smiled indulgently at Rutt. 'That leaves the toad and those who'll come to see it. It all depends on how wide this disaster's been. If the whole of Zuzubia's in a state of emergency, they'll probably stay away. But is that likely? This is a flood, caused by a river overflowing its banks. It was raining here for weeks before the flood suddenly came. What caused it was surely high up in the mountains hundreds of miles east of here. So although no one's been able to get to us, and we haven't been able to get to them, the disaster may not be affecting most of the rest of Zuzubia at all. Stanley, what are you doing?'

Stanley was holding his fork vertically in front of his face. On either side, Kirsten could see his eyes focussing on the object in front of him. But it wasn't the fork or his eyes that transfixed her. A round, brown sac, a little smaller than a golf ball, seemed to have replaced Stanley's nose. At first she wasn't sure. The candlelight was playing tricks, making the thing look bigger than perhaps it was. She peered closer. With a sense of growing dread which became a certainty, Kirsten knew what was on top of Stanley's fork. It was the stewed scrotum of the male Scrotum Toad. Words could not escape her lips. She stood up, glided sideways out of the door and flew up the track towards her house. She'd gone before she could hear Jake say, 'Now we know what the toad likes: onions and gravy.' Nor could Kirsten hear Tangle squeaking, 'The stores. I never showed Kwame the stores. It was that blasted generator. Kwame must have mistaken…'

Lola finished her sentence for her. 'Kirsten's specimens for a living larder.'

Kirsten flung herself amongst her cages. The toads had gone, both sexes. So had the Central African Mud Turtle. And where was the *Lycodonomorphus*?

Back in the dining room, Teeny was attempting to comfort Tangle. 'Oh, don't worry about it. You couldn't have known that Kwame was only a waiter. The most important thing was the stew. It was absolutely delicious, even if it does make me feel a bit queasy thinking what was in it.'

As usual, Jake had the last word. 'Think, Teeny, it might have been Witty the Fourth.' Granville found himself reluctantly thinking about baby Benjamin. Tangle was silently weeping. Stanley was noisily retching.

CHAPTER TWENTY-TWO

The sound of a helicopter made them jump up from the breakfast table. They sprinted, straggled, or hobbled according to their fitness until they could get a clear view to the south, all except Kirsten, who'd failed to appear that morning. The helicopter was landing on the only cleared area within a mile, down at the bottom of a steepish track. Chest, Teeny and Stanley, the last to arrive, could see Tangle standing rigid as though waiting for some terrible answer to a question she dared not ask.

A door opened and out stepped what looked like a lone African Chief in full ceremonial regalia. He crouched low until he was clear of the blades, straightened and looked about him. To their surprise, the helicopter rose, tilted forward and shot off to the south leaving the great man staring up at them. As he started climbing the hill, they could see that he wore sandals, a leopard skin pillbox *kofia* for a hat and long robes of purple and green which they called a *grand boubou* in West Africa. The sense of grandeur was enhanced by an elegant fly whisk. He reached the brow of the hill and stood facing the welcoming party as though the guest of honour at an investiture.

'Well, ain't this the backside of nowhere. Who's the big dealer round here?'

'If you mean who's in charge,' said Mo, 'it's Ms Tangwystl Breeze here.'

The man looked surprised, Tangle terrified.

'A donna?' He walked up to Tangle, then round her, as though inspecting a prize heifer at a show. Jake wondered if he'd be able to control himself if the man prodded her with his fly whisk. Stanley thought he must be the most important man in Zuzubia, perhaps the President himself. But the others weren't fooled. That voice had given him away.

'Who are you?' asked Granville suspiciously.

The man suddenly stopped stalking Tangle and marched up to Granville. 'Hey, you look like ya shit don't smell. You sure is biggified.' He sniffed and flicked his whisk. 'Since you ask, my name for those who don't already know it is Bumpin' Gully, King of the Gangsta Flow. I make lip music, I sure am good, I'm bustin' out, that's understood.'

'What are you doing here and what do you want?' Gully gave a sideways leap from Granville to Mo.

'How very kind of you to ask. I just thought I'd slide by and peep things out.' He gave a leering smile.

Mo stood his ground. 'Where have you come from?'

'Kum-ba-la. Kum-ba-la.'

'But you're not from there. Let me guess. Bronx?'

'Queens born and raised.'

Mo was getting impatient. It was an important day for all of them and this was a side show. 'What do you want?'

Bumpin' Gully smiled, but it wasn't a nice smile. 'Why you coppin' an attitude?' He started to walk away in no particular direction then spun back to face them. 'I've come to greet my fellow bloods, or shall I say one of them.'

Lola was quickest on the uptake. 'You're tracing your ancestors. You think your people come from here, so you've come to find them. That's beautiful.'

Gully turned towards her and beamed. 'What have we here? A blue-eyed soul sister?'

Lola, whose eyes were brown, knew what he meant. She delighted in someone who didn't speak or act normal. 'I like it,' she purred. 'A conceptual realisation of the alter ego. An organic narrative rendering an ethnicity gesture.'

To Gully, Lola looked like a cuddle-bunny who'd been round the track. But this was too much. 'You trying to blow smoke up my ass, lady?'

Lola enjoyed confusing people. To her, obfuscation was the highest form of Art. She was thrilled to find someone who slipped so easily into gobbledegook. Tangle had been a great discovery and now here was another one.

'What's it like in Kumbala?' Chest thundered.

'No need to crank it up. Woo-hoo-hoo.' Gully put

a finger in an ear and waggled it theatrically. 'Kumbala's creepsville.'

'But what's it like between there and here?' asked Granville, trying not to sound exasperated.

'Bushy-bushy. Nothing there.'

'What about the floods?'

'What floods?'

They all gasped. Was this man real or simply a joker? Granville persisted. 'You're not trying to tell us that you haven't seen or heard about the floods, are you?'

'Say, you're so airified I can feel your bitch. I'm tellin' you all, I seen no flood. I flew into Kumbala two days ago, decked myself out in bling fly for this turf, conversated some big willie and hired a chopper. No one said nothin' about no flood.'

Tangle decided it was time to assert her authority. 'Well, Mr Gully, welcome to *Waters of Eostre*. Why don't we all go inside and have a nice cup of tea and talk about it?'

'Chill, lady. I mistook you for a boopety hunkamo. You're one cool sister. I'm cocked and ready to go.'

There was still no sign of Kirsten as they sat down to tea and coffee. Jake made them all jump by banging his fist on the table, rattling the crockery and spilling some drinks, which earned a rebuke from Tangle. 'I know you, you're the guy who had that hit, what was it, the one where the monkeys take their clothes off and the girls don't. That was great. What was it called?'

'I think you referring to *Whipping the Game*. Yo bitch, you real homeboy.'

Jake turned to the others. 'For those of you who don't know it, the message is sexual frustration. The words promise sex but the action doesn't.'

To Jake's delight, Gully obliged with a short burst. 'Gee mo nitty, the feelin' ain't pretty, I was boned out dry and that's no lie; now I'm all hogged up like an overflowin' cup; what Charley needs now is a double-master blaster and a grand finale.'

Jake couldn't help himself. 'You indiscreet, in de street.'

Gully gave him a sharp glance, then the benefit of the doubt. 'You gotta let ya nutz hang, guts bang, bang like a hammer, be cock of the game.'

'That's right, Gully, go for it, show them what you're really like.'

'I ain't no wimp, I ain't no punk, got a gangsta limp; when I get rappin' I don't fake the funk.' Gully paused, staring hard at Rutt. 'Hey, don't I know you some place?'

Like Jake, Rutt had recognised Gully. He'd been frustrated that his own fame, which was greater than Gully's, hadn't been acknowledged.

'Rutt's the greatest actor in the world,' Teeny cried out. Rutt, who'd been wondering how to respond to Gully, decided to leave it at that. He hadn't noticed Lola's sneer.

'After Gully,' Jake added impishly. As if to confirm this, Gully rose to his feet and started punching the air, much to Tangle's alarm. 'I'm so cooled out I whip the game; stand in my way and you'll feel the pain; I got faith, you got no hope, charity begins at home, it's dope.'

This won Teeny over. 'That's so wonderful to hear, Mr Gully. I'm so pleased that you've got Faith. It's been sadly lacking around here.' She shot a bitter glance at Lola who returned it in kind. 'Does this mean that you're a True Believer?'

'God's my big-hitter, now don't you titter, my faith it just gets fitter and fitter.'

'Yes,' cried Teeny. She was almost weeping with relief.

Chest put a hand on her arm. 'You tell 'em, Honeybunnikins.'

'You're getting all of a doodah,' said Jake impertinently.

'Hasn't this all gone a bit far?' Granville's face was as acid as his voice.

'You creep me out, Mr Bad-Eye.'

'Please!' Tangle wailed.

Mo intervened. 'Will you let me explain our situation, Gully? We've been cut off from the rest of Zuzubia for nearly a week. Half the people you see here are those who live and work here. The rest escaped from a disaster at a game lodge eight miles upriver. A sudden and terrible flood washed away their hotel. There was considerable loss of life.'

'Hellified shit!'

'So you see when we heard a helicopter we hoped it was coming to rescue us. We were all shocked when it took off again. That's why we've been at cross-purposes.'

To Mo's irritation, Jake took over. 'There's

another reason why we had the abdabs. One of our party,' he peered melodramatically around the room, 'who isn't here, has made a fabulous discovery. She found a long-extinct toad and his wife which hadn't been seen for sixty years.'

'I found the wife,' said Stanley.

'You did, Stanley. She was humungous, but her husband was the eye popper. You see he had the most enormous scrotum.'

'Jake, I don't think this is a priority.' Mo's attempt to steer the conversation back to important issues was ignored by Jake.

'These discoveries were so big they were making Kirsten famous. We've been expecting hordes of people to arrive to inspect them. But then we ate them.'

'Oh Jake!' Tangle cried in despair.

Gully looked incredulous and then suspicious. 'Who you ate?'

'The toads, not the people. We had them in a stew last night. Come to think of it, are we really sure what Kwame put in that pot? I expect he's preparing lunch now. I wonder where Kirsten is? Perhaps we're having Danish casserole. Anyhow, back to last night. There was definitely a turtle, a snake, the toads and Mr Toad's scrotum.'

For reasons not appreciated by most of them, Gully found this as hilarious as Jake had intended. 'You ate a toad's winky bag? Straight heavy! I'm cracked up.'

Granville had had enough of this. 'Did you see any evidence in Kumbala that anyone's coming to rescue us?'

To say that Gully had taken a dislike to Granville was like saying the Pope mildly disapproved of sin. 'You givin' me the coke stare, honkie? Why you hatin' on a cool-daddy? You need to keep your dick in your pants.'

Mo tried to smooth things over. 'Perhaps we can help you find your ancestor? What have you found out already?'

Gully gave a deep sigh. 'When some slick-boy from Harlem told me my folks came from this part of Africa, I thought he was big-assing me. But when he said he could prove I was related to one of the biggest players in Zuzubia I had to break shit.'

'If I understand you right,' said Mo tentatively, 'you've come here to *Waters of Eostre* to see an important person who you think may be your relative?

'You're on the real.'

'So what makes you think he's here?'

'Slow your roll. He ain't here.'

'So why come here?'

'To greet a brother. He's on his way, left early this morning.'

Tangle gave a jerk of terror. Anyone coming this way was one too many for her.

'How do you know?' asked Granville.

'You again. You still givin' me the bad-lip, honkie?'

Mo had to step in again. 'You say this important person is on his way? To here?'

'That's what his ass-lickers told me. They said do a homo and blow out Kumbala, get yourself to

Waters of Eostre faster than you can pop your cookies. He'll greet you there.'

'Who will?'

'My long-lost cousin. They tell me he's the mutt's nuts. Do anything for a fellow blood.'

'What's his name?'

'Godson. Godson Malembe. Say he's the Minister of Finance.'

Tangle let out a sob, Mo a snort, Stanley a kind of humph and Jake a slow ha, ha, ha. Kirsten, had she been there, might have turned yellow.

CHAPTER TWENTY-THREE

Kirsten awoke to that heaviness felt when something unpleasant has happened. Within seconds the events of the previous evening crashed down on her like a breaking wave. She felt sick at the thought of her dead toads, turtle and snake but couldn't make up her mind whether the special loss of the toads made it worse. They'd been her triumph, yet what in reality had she done? An Obooboan had found one and Stanley the other. The toads had been nothing but trouble. She'd only ever wanted to be a zoologist; the life of a celebrity would never have suited her.

Was she angry? No, just depressed. She'd heard the sound of a helicopter arriving and leaving, but felt she didn't want to be involved in whatever it was.

She could so easily blame Kwame, but he'd done nothing malicious. Tangle? Yes, it had been careless of her not to have instructed Kwame properly, but how could Kirsten be angry with someone who'd done so much for her? She loved Tangle, everyone did; the word was not too strong. She needed closure, and for that she needed to heal herself through the act of forgiveness. Merely thinking to herself that she forgave Kwame was not enough. She needed to offer herself to him and for him to forgive her too. And when she'd achieved that, she would want their reconciliation to be declared publicly, with Kwame's endorsement. That was the only way she could face Tangle and the others.

Kwame, still suffering from the loss of Madam and his unsuccessful journey here to find her, was in turmoil. He'd been moved by Ms Breeze's kindness the previous evening and had been relieved to find employment. When he'd been told that he'd done something which these strange people seemed to regard as terrible, he'd expected retribution, at the very least to be fired. Ms Breeze had told him that what he'd done was bad, but she'd said it calmly without blame or rancour. And she hadn't dismissed him, at least not yet. He wasn't sure what was expected of him, so he hung around, not daring to return to the house but skulking in the trees. He'd seen the *muzungu* swarm out at the sound of the helicopter, but now they'd all disappeared inside the house again. So he peered through the undergrowth at the only person he could see, the youngest of the ladies, the one whose animals he'd put into the stew.

Now that Kirsten had carried out a more thorough stock take than had been possible in the dark, nothing more seemed to be missing. She was just checking the last of the outside cages when she was aware of someone watching her. She looked up and saw an African through the trees. It was Kwame. Slowly she straightened. With her head on one side and her hands spread forward like a Madonna holding the infant Christ in a Renaissance painting, she gently closed a finger in a beckoning gesture. Kwame, who'd rocked onto the balls of his feet ready to bolt, became mesmerised by Kirsten's silent insistence. Slowly his legs started walking towards her without him telling them to. She smiled as he drew near and it seemed they might actually embrace. Kwame stopped.

'It is all right,' she whispered. 'All will be good. Come with me, let us show them at the house that you will forgive me.'

Kwame's eyes widened. What strange words. She is not saying that she needs to forgive me, but that I should forgive her. I do not know why, but here is another lovely lady. He managed to flicker a half-smile in return.

To his surprise she took his hand. 'You and me,' was all she said as they started walking down the track. He stole a glance down her front. She wasn't fat like Madam, but she wasn't skinny either. She made him feel comfortable. Her tiny hand was soft in his own. He was disappointed when she gave a little squeeze and let go.

Chairs scraped as Mo and Jake leapt to their feet, followed more slowly by Granville, Rutt and a teeth-gritting Chest. Of the men, only Gully and Stanley remained seated with Tangle, Teeny and Lola. Mo tried to usher Kirsten to his seat, but she hung back, guiding a reluctant Kwame into the centre of the room. She didn't seem to have noticed Gully.

'I want you all to know that what happened last night is for the best. The toads have gone, so our problems go with them. Living here has made me realise that friendship and loyalty mean more than owning things. When something goes wrong, it is how people react that is important. I have known such incredible generosity here and have been made to feel part of a family. I include Joseph, who I hope and pray is safe and will return to us soon. I cannot hide my feelings for him. He is one of the most remarkable men I have ever met. And now I have a new friend. When Tangle and Jake had to work on the generator last night, and Kwame was told to prepare our dinner, he used his initiative without fuss.' She turned to face him. 'Kwame, can you be my friend?'

Kwame attempted a smile, distorted by confusion. 'Yes, Madam.'

This was too much for Tangle, who swept up to Kirsten and embraced her. She turned to Kwame with a 'what the heck' look and flung her arms round him too.

'Well, don't that beat all,' boomed Chest.

But before they could talk further of forgiveness and love, they were distracted by events outside. Only the young ears of Jake could hear it at first. Kirsten was far too engrossed, but gradually Rutt and Lola could be seen, mouths agape and eyes locked, listening to a sound which would soon be picked up by the others. A steady roar was starting to rattle the windows. Jake ran to the door. 'Sounds like they're coming,' he called over his shoulder as he rushed out, followed by Stanley. One after the other they tumbled and tottered out of the house, just as they'd done an hour earlier when first hearing the clacking of a helicopter. Only Gully and Kwame remained.

A persistent rumble was swelling in the direction of the river. It sounded like a large convoy grinding up the hill towards *Waters of Eostre*. On it growled until an army truck tipped over the brow of the hill followed by another, two, three, four… Mo counted seven in all. They stopped in line inches from one another. A lone soldier, a big bear of a man, jumped down from the cab of the third truck and held the door open. An even vaster figure started to climb out. They could see sergeant's stripes on the shoulder of the first man, whose salute had to be abandoned quickly when Godson Malembe, for it was he, missed his footing on the last step and tottered backwards. The sergeant caught him expertly, to Jake's disappointment, although he couldn't suppress a giggle. Tangle hissed at him. Malembe brushed down his shoulders as though he'd been contaminated, glaring at the sergeant like it had been his fault.

Nobody else moved. Whoever was in the trucks remained there. Lola found herself listening to a bird trilling away exotically to their left. It seemed no one wanted to do anything until it had finished.

A door opened in the fourth truck. Tangle let out a gasp as she saw Garston Peters carefully climb down from the cab. He walked self-consciously up to Malembe and the sergeant, trying not to look up at Tangle and the others. Malembe eyed him derisively. The three of them, Malembe, the sergeant and Peters, waddled, marched and shuffled forward until they stood a few metres from the residents of *Waters of Eostre*. Mo couldn't help noting the similarity with the situation an hour previously when they'd stood in a line facing Gully.

Malembe said something to the sergeant, who let out a thunderclap of a bark which made them all jump. Soldiers burst from the rear of all seven vehicles; there must have been fifty of them. They fanned out in a large arc behind Malembe, all except five who disconcertingly took up positions behind Tangle and the others. At a further command from the sergeant, all the soldiers stamped and presented their rifles angled inwards towards the centre. Teeny whimpered.

Malembe lifted his head and looked disdainfully down his nose at them. Peters had said there would be five Europeans at most, three men and two women. There were actually ten altogether, six men and four women. He wondered why, but it didn't bother him.

'So this is the place,' he sneered. 'I have heard so much about it.' He paused for effect, then shook his head vigorously. 'None of it good.' He looked from Lola to Tangle to Kirsten to Teeny, giving Kirsten a particularly nasty grimace. So, she thought, he's recognised me. 'Which one of you is called Tantle Bruise?' Peters started to correct him but subsided under a shrivelling glance. Tangle tried to reply but her voice had locked in terror. Timidly she raised a drooping hand.

'So. You. What kind of a place do you think you can run here in Zuzubia? Do you think we are a soft touch? Do you think you are still living in colonial times that you can take us for fools?' A corner of his mouth curled up taking a nostril with it. 'Are you a Zuzubian citizen that you think you can take away the livelihood of poor people who work the soil?'

Mo was praying that Jake would for once keep his trap shut, but even Jake was cowed by all those rifles, especially the ones behind.

'This place stinks. It is a place of rotting defilement. A suppuration on the honest face of Zuzubia.' He shuffled closer to Tangle. He smelt her fear and she his breath. He inspected all parts of her face. 'We should make an example here. You deserve to be punished.' A horrible smile, the smile of the accomplished bully, spread across his face. 'Now let me see. This has to be…' he paused as though searching for the word, 'appropriate. Something that people will remember for a long time. Ah, but you are a woman.' He brightened. 'And I am a gentleman.' He leered at her. 'I will return to you.' That ghastly smile again. He stepped back and looked around. 'Which of you is Moshe Guterman?'

'I am,' said Mo coolly.

Malembe peered at him. He'd seen a blurred photo of the person said to have been controlling the public address system at the food eating competition. The man before him didn't look anything like that, not surprisingly as Mo had been wearing a blond wig and false moustache at the time. 'You,' he jabbed a finger at Mo, 'are wanted on charges of espionage and subversion.'

Then charge me, Mo wanted to fire back at him, but he knew better than to open his mouth.

'I will return to you as well.' Malembe nodded slowly. Now he addressed his whole audience. 'I am here on the business of the Republic of Zuzubia. I am the Minister of Finance. The Very Honourable Mr Godson Malembe is my name. Ah, but some of you already know that. His eyes passed up and down the row of people. There is one person here who has committed a serious crime.' He raised his voice. 'An even more serious crime. Treason! It is my duty to bring that person to justice. But in this case it is also personal. I am only human.'

'I doubt that,' muttered Granville under his breath.

'I am not a vengeful man.' Again the sinister smile. 'But when someone tries to poison me,' he surveyed the members of his audience in turn, deliberately leaving Kirsten until last, 'can you blame me when I become an angry man? This person I know. This person I have seen. The poisoner!'

None of them took in the sound of a distant helicopter.

When the others had rushed out of the house, Kwame had found himself standing alone in front of a man who looked like an important African, but not from these parts. He must be from some foreign tribe, he thought. He certainly spoke foreign.

'Yo, blood, whadup? You's da cock o' da hood?'

Gully advanced on Kwame and punched him lightly on the chest. 'Chillax. You bustin' tight. You 'n' me we gotta stick together. How's about you 'n' me besties?' Kwame smiled nervously at him. 'Say, what these folks really like?'

It was the first thing Gully had said which Kwame understood. 'They good people. The ladies, they kind.'

Gully winked at Kwame. 'You like the ladies, hah? How come you like the ladies?'

'They been good to me.' Kwame let it all pour out, how he'd been attracted to Madam at *Crowned Crane Lodge*, how disaster had struck, how he'd been traumatised by seeing Madam floating down the river and how he'd thought she might have survived and come to this rock. He told Gully of his terrifying journey and his grief when he'd discovered that Madam wasn't here. He described how Tangle had welcomed him in and offered him a job as cook. He recounted what had happened with the stew and how Tangle had been gentle with him and had forgiven him. He explained how the toads belonged to Kirsten and she'd forgiven him too, as Gully had witnessed. 'The ladies, they kind,' he repeated.

'Tru dat, coke's your phat, cool by me dat.' He gave Kwame a sympathetic smile. 'Check this out. I have a dream, a mission, and I mean to fulfil. This your turf, me I'm just visitin'. I got juice all round the world. They call me Bumpin' Gully. But here, not my hood. I need your game, you 'n' me in the mix, funked up, cut buddies. How's that hang?'

His words were unintelligible but his tone was friendly. Kwame smiled back at him.

Gully looked towards the open door. 'There's some wild noise goin' on out there.' He picked up his fly whisk. 'C'mon, let's spit the funk.' He slung his robes over his shoulder, put a hand on Kwame's back, and swept him out the room.

They glanced in the direction of a helicopter which they could hear cutting its engines down by the river, but could see nothing through the trees. Halfway across the dirt to where Malembe was haranguing Kirsten, they had to pass between two soldiers. Kwame hung back, but Gully tugged him forward, tossing a 'Chill, blood!' over his shoulder as he passed. They stood to the side of Stanley, drinking in the scene. Gully observed the ring of soldiers, the burly sergeant, the obese figure of Malembe and the shifty looking Garston Peters. It was only when he heard Malembe proudly repeat that he was the Minister of Finance that Gully realised he was looking at his cousin. He was about to introduce himself when Malembe took a step forward and put his nose inches from Kirsten's.

'I know you. Do you think I wouldn't remember you? Did you think your poison would make me forget? To poison a Minister of the Republic of Zuzubia is treason! You made me drink your poison. Now the boot is on the other foot. You will come with me and I will make you drink mine.' He took a pace back and said something to his sergeant, who cocked his rifle and started to advance on Kirsten.

Rutt moved. He moved so fast that Lola never saw him move, only that he was suddenly there in front of Kirsten. He was there long before Teeny could have said, 'Do something, Rutt, save us like you did in *Facing the Onslaught*!' and Granville might have said, 'He's an actor, you stupid woman, and that was a film.' It took courage for Rutt to place himself between Kirsten and a giant with a loaded rifle supported by fifty others. But Rutt did more than that. He not only shielded Kirsten, but did it in such a way that his action didn't seem aggressive. As he'd thrown himself between the sergeant and Kirsten, Rutt had flung his hands above his head in a gesture of non-violence in the classic position of surrender. And as every footballer who'd stood in the wall facing a free kick knew, not putting your hands in a protecting position didn't come naturally. Wow, thought Jake, that takes balls, though even he couldn't smirk at the unintended pun.

'Know who I am?' Rutt was shielding Kirsten from the sergeant but addressing Malembe. 'You get your hand offa my girlfriend or the whole world's a-gonna hear 'bout it.'

'He's the biggest movie star in the world,' squeaked Teeny, 'and the best.'

'Yer, an' I'm runnin' for the Congress of the US of A. You wait 'til the Tea Party gets to hear o' this. They'll be all riled up, mad as cut snakes.'

'Touch Rutt Revere and his woman,' Chest joined in, 'and you'll be headline news from New York to Sydney. My President will be on the blower to yours before you've stepped back into that truck.' He hobbled up to join Rutt, knocking the sergeant's rifle as he passed. 'I'm Hollywood's greatest movie producer. You can't do piddlee-o without me and my contacts putting your name around the world. I'll give you the greatest starring role Africa's ever seen, and you won't be playing Nelson Mandela, you'd better believe it. And one more thing, Mister. My friend Mo Guterman here, he's worked for some of the biggest networks in the world: CNN and the BBC. Lay a finger on him and your President will be asking you why Zuzubia has become headline news from Puerto Rico to Beijing.'

Now Lola stepped forward. 'And I'm the world's leading authority on modern art. I've commissioned some of the most notorious exhibitions in the last twenty years. If you don't do what he says, the world's going to be queuing up to see my latest piece of kinetic art: you strung up by your bollocks.'

It was Granville's turn. 'I'm a world-renowned surgeon whose operations are legendary. But mark my words, I'm not going to sew the aforementioned organs back on when you do finally drop down.'

Jake had been wondering how he might contribute. 'And I'm big in rubber.'

Stanley was feeling out of it too. 'I'm big Kev and I'm the meanest man on TV.'

Jake supported him. 'That's right, he is. Millions tune in every night to watch Big Kev. I'm terrified of him.'

Malembe rounded on Peters. 'You never told me all these people were here.'

'I didn't know,' wailed Peters.

'He would say that,' shouted Jake.

As one of those accused by Malembe, Mo had thought it best if he remained silent. But he had his wits about him sufficiently to notice that the one person who hadn't been defended was Tangle. 'You can forget any plans to touch Ms Breeze or harm this beautiful place, Mr Malembe. She employs many Zuzubians at *Waters of Eostre* and treats them well. They love working for her. She protects the environment, provides sustainable food for the people of Zuzubia, and accommodation and assistance to Kirsten here, a distinguished zoologist who has made a great discovery. The real problem is that man.' Mo walked up to Garston Peters. He called back to Malembe over his shoulder. 'You've heard my friends here. They're all powerful people, the biggest movie star in the world, the greatest film producer, a world famous surgeon and a renowned sponsor of the arts.' Mo thought it best if he left Jake and Stanley out of it. 'They've told you how you can save yourself by leaving us alone. But that won't be enough. This man is corrupt from the top of his head to the soles of his feet. If you don't make sure he never comes near this place again, if you don't make sure that he has no influence over *Waters of Eostre* whatsoever, if you don't treat him as the criminal which he is, then your name will appear linked to his in lights all around the world.'

Gully had heard enough. He'd come all this way to meet his cousin. Kwame had convinced him that these honkies were ace. The sight of these poor folks being bum-fingered by this poop-butt was shit-ass. 'Why you hatin' on these people? Iz you trazy? Why you dissin' these good folks, dem's ma friends, na mean?'

Malembe had been checked by all the white people and the power they'd displayed. Now he was puzzled as to why this African Chief was addressing him aggressively in a foreign tongue. His confusion allowed Gully to continue. 'You playin' da wrong riff, boots. What's your beef? Whadup with all dem bloods strapped and bucked, ready to go off? You, the Great-Grandson of Paramount Chief Nadikolu, same as me?'

For the first time Malembe understood a little of what Gully had said. He remembered now that he'd been told that a distant cousin was coming out from the USA to meet him. Malembe held out his hand. Gully did more than reject it. He fluttered his fly whisk in Malembe's face. The sergeant stepped forward cocking his rifle. Gully ignored him. 'I thought you was ace. You think you're all that but you ain't. Our Great Grand-Daddy Nadikolu would be shittin' hisself if he could see you now, fasho.'

———

Shane Dunster paused when he saw the soldiers surrounding the huddled group at the top of the hill. Although fit, he was puffed after the steep climb up from his helicopter down by the river. He took in the ring of armed men, the ten or so white people and, at the front, the unmistakable bulk of the Minister of Finance communing with a clown who looked as though he was in panto.

Shane marched up to Malembe and greeted him heartily. 'G'day, Minister, what a beaut. I trust you're in good nick?' Gully and Malembe broke off at the sheer brazenness of the interruption. 'I've just been having brekkie with the President. He sends his regards. He's asked me to pass on several messages. He's requested you do me the honour of opening my new health centre in a month's time. The Pressie can't make it himself, off to a conference in Abu Dhabi or some such place. Oh, and he's asked me to give you this.'

'What is it?' asked Malembe suspiciously.

'DVD of the food eating competition. Told me to tell you to have a butcher's.'

'Has he seen it himself?' If Malembe was looking worried, that was nothing to the expression on Garston Peters' face.

'You bet. We watched it together this morning. He was gobsmacked.'

'What did he say?'

'Good onya, mate, or words to that effect. At the end he said, 'Leave it to me, I'll deal with the people responsible for this.' Shane turned to Peters with a cool stare. 'Or maybe I got that wrong. He didn't say the people responsible; he said the person. That's it, that's what he said, the person responsible for this.' He turned back to Malembe. 'It's pretty darned obvious who he's referring to.' Malembe looked blankly at him. 'It will be when you've watched the DVD, Minister. It'll stand out like a dog's balls, won't it Mr Peters?'

Shane looked round. He nodded a greeting to Mo and his eyes were inevitably drawn to the exotic figure of Gully. He turned to Lola hopefully. 'And which of you ladies calls herself Tangwystl Breeze?'

This time Tangle could speak. 'It's me.'

'I've got a message from the President for you too. Says he's heard of all the good things you've been doing here and would like to pay you a visit sometime soon.'

Tangle choked. 'It would be an honour.'

Granville stepped forward and addressed Malembe. 'If I may say so, Sir, it sounds as though your President is a wise man. He has understood the good work which Ms Breeze is doing here, and the valuable roles played by Mr Guterman and the others at *Waters of Eostre*. We came here in a terrible state escaping from a disaster. Ms Breeze and her colleagues saved us and welcomed us, and I hope I speak for all my fellow guests from *Crowned Crane Lodge* when I say that *Waters of Eostre* has made us proud to have visited your country. We will speak well of Zuzubia when we return home.'

'You bet,' hollered Chest.

'It seems, Sir,' Granville continued carefully, 'that your only problem rests with this gentleman here.' He cocked an eyebrow at Garston Peters.

Malembe took the hint. He spoke rapidly to his sergeant. Jake, Tangle and Mo were slightly disappointed that he didn't arrest Peters on the spot and frogmarch him back to his truck. But, Mo reflected, he hadn't seen the DVD yet. Instead, the sergeant snapped a command which sent his soldiers rushing back to their trucks like a film in reverse. It was left to Malembe himself to cuff Peters hard on the shoulder and the sergeant to heave Malembe into the cab.

When the last of the trucks had tipped over the brow of the hill, Jake let out a great whoop and the hugging started. Teeny was reconciled with Lola, and Gully with Granville. Everyone linked arms and jigged in a circle like a huddle of victorious footballers, legs kicking out the back. Gully peered round and saw Kwame watching them. He pulled him in and they danced on, laughing and screaming like children.

I do hope that you've enjoyed *The Scrotum Toad*. I'd be delighted if you would take the time to leave a review on Amazon. Reviews are so important to authors, and do not have to be too long or detailed. Just a word to say that you liked the book would be very much appreciated.

Charles Moberly

viewauthor.at/CharlesMoberly

Also by Charles Moberly...

The Corncrake

The four members of an Anglo-German family are loving and close-knit. But there are tensions between Richard, a vicar, and his son Tristram. They clash over religion, farming practices and the treatment of Tristram's sister, Adela.

The onset of the First World War brings new pressures. Untrue stories of German atrocities, invented by irresponsible newspapers, stir up hatred of Germans living in Britain, and force the government to enact harsh laws.

The Hall family is torn between a desire for mutual protection and their very different attitudes towards what is happening to them personally and in the wider context around them.

The Corncrake is a historical novel set in 1909-10 and 1914-15, when pacifism is confronted by the Church of England's endorsement of the glories of sacrifice for God, King and Country.

Coming soon...

***Try the Leopard's Mouth* by Charles Moberly**

Briony and Tom, both in their late twenties, are very different characters. But opposites attract, and in business as in love they complement each other well.

The onset of the Rhodesian - Zimbabwean War of Independence tears at the couple's relationship. Misunderstandings arise from their respective personalities and from external pressures. Events pull them apart, but also bind them together.

Try the Leopard's Mouth is a romantic thriller set in Africa. But it is also a historical novel, grounded in real events in the period 1970-80.

Printed in Great Britain
by Amazon

35302609R00152